SEEING SHADOWS

Lexie Brookes is busy running her hairdressing salon and wondering what to do about her cooling relationship with her partner, Danny. When the jewellery shop next door is broken into via her own premises, the owner — the wealthy and infuriatingly arrogant Bruno Cavendish — blames her for his losses. Then Danny disappears, and Lexie is suddenly targeted by a mysterious stalker. To add to the turmoil, Bruno appears to be attracted to her, and she finds herself equally drawn to him . . .

Books by Susan Udy
in the Linford Romance Library:

THE CALL OF THE PEACOCK
FORTUNE'S BRIDE
DARK FORTUNE
DANGEROUS LEGACY
REBELLIOUS HEARTS
SUSPICIOUS HEART
TENDER TAKEOVER
DARK SUSPICION
CLIFF HOUSE
THE UNFORGIVING HEART
THE RELUCTANT STAND-IN
I'M WATCHING YOU
FLIGHT OF THE HERON
A TENDER CONFLICT
FRANCESCA
TROUBLE IN PARADISE
THE SHADOW IN THE DARK

SUSAN UDY

SEEING SHADOWS

Complete and Unabridged

LINFORD
Leicester

First published in Great Britain in 2017

First Linford Edition
published 2017

A catalogue record for this book is available from the British Library.

ISBN 978–1–4448–3187–0

Published by
F. A. Thorpe (Publishing)
Anstey, Leicestershire

Set by Words & Graphics Ltd.
Anstey, Leicestershire
Printed and bound in Great Britain by
T. J. International Ltd., Padstow, Cornwall

This book is printed on acid-free paper

1

Lexie Brookes stood on the pavement in front of her hairdressing salon, Clever Cuts, and stared at the door. The glass had been smashed, yet it didn't look as if anyone had actually opened it and been inside. She frowned and slid the key into the lock. Before she'd even started to turn it, the door opened, scraping noisily over the shards of glass lying on the floor inside. It must have been left slightly ajar; so slightly, it hadn't been noticeable from outside. Vandals, content to simply smash the glass? In which case, why reach in and open the door?

Gingerly, Lexie picked her way through the broken glass and went inside. At first glance, nothing appeared to be missing. Everything was in its proper place. She frowned and strode between the line of washbasins and chairs against one wall and the row of hood hairdryers opposite them before going into the small staffroom to remove her jacket and hang it up. Once inside, it became glaringly obvious why the door had been opened. A hole, big enough for a man to climb through, had been knocked through the wall directly into the shop next door.

'Oh no,' Lexie breathed. No wonder the thieves hadn't bothered stealing anything from her salon — not when they'd managed to break through into Cavendish Gems and its considerably richer pickings.

For Cavendish Gems was a very exclusive jewellery shop, one of a nationwide chain of twenty, and which only sold the most expensive items; breathtakingly expensive, in fact. Clearly, the impregnable steel shutters that were fitted over its windows and door made entry via Lexie's salon the only way in.

She didn't bother trying to look through the hole. Instead, she pulled her mobile phone from her handbag and dialled 999. 'Police,' she then said to the call handler at the other end of the line. She was surprised that no one had reported her broken glass door. Because if they had, wouldn't the police have informed her? Not that there were many people about at this time of the morning; and the few that she'd passed had, for the most part, looked preoccupied with their own business. Whatever, no one had taken the time to investigate; probably assuming, like she had initially, that the damage had been inflicted by vandals. And with no visible signs of a break-in at the front of Cavendish Gems, it wouldn't have been apparent what had happened.

Lexie had decided to come in early before any of her staff members arrived, so it was only just eight o'clock. She'd intended to spend an hour catching up with her accounting before opening at nine. It was a task she loathed and invariably put off for as long as she could. But with things in danger of getting too far behind, she'd decided to make use of a quiet hour and catch up. Now, of course, that wouldn't happen.

Two plainclothes policemen

— detectives, she assumed — arrived fairly promptly, and she showed them the damage in the staffroom. They poked their heads through the hole as far as they could, but didn't linger. Instead, they returned to the pavement outside where they stood, regarding the untouched exterior of Cavendish Gems and murmuring in low tones to each other.

'Right,' one of them finally said, 'we'd better get in touch with the owner.'

The words had no sooner left their lips when a youngish, smartly dressed man arrived and stared curiously at them. 'Can I help you?' he asked. He then noticed the smashed glass in the salon door. 'Oh dear. Problems?'

Lexie knew he wasn't the manager — that was Simon Hartnell, and he was considerably older than this man. Simon would be in his fifties, she guessed. He was a punctiliously polite man — charming even, whenever their paths crossed, which wasn't often. This man must be a member of his staff. Yet, she couldn't remember having seen him before. But then, why would she have? She'd never had any reason to enter the shop, the prices being way beyond her means.

It was the same with the owner of the place, Bruno Cavendish; she'd only glimpsed him once or twice. Even so, she'd gained a fleeting impression of a tall, handsome man midway through his thirties, she would have said, with a powerful build and a head of thick hair the colour of oiled teak. They'd never as much as spoken; and although he lived in Adlington, she'd never ever seen him round town. But then again, he probably only frequented the more exclusive parts — the parts that contained the select wine bars, the expensive restaurants, the places where the rich and powerful tended to congregate. In any case, she wasn't sure she'd recognise him.

One of the detectives wasted no time in informing the man of what had taken place overnight. He looked horrified and immediately began the process of unlocking, a procedure which took several minutes due to the steel shutters and complicated security locks, before he all but ran into the shop.

'Oh my God,' he moaned as the blood literally drained from his face, leaving it the exact shade of putty.

The detectives followed him in, as did Lexie, although she only took one step inside. Nonetheless, she could see what had happened. Display cabinets were empty but looked as if they were still locked, their contents being more valuable and so kept secure overnight somewhere else, she guessed. But racks that would most likely have held cheaper items had been stripped bare, and the glass-topped counter was also empty. The man then muttered 'The safe,' and ignoring the detectives' cautionary words about contaminating possible evidence, hastened into a back room. The two detectives followed him, so Lexie decided it would be okay to do the same.

Again, it was obvious what had happened. This was where the thieves had broken in via the hole. She saw a large safe, which she assumed would have contained the most precious pieces, its door standing open, its contents obviously gone.

'Everything's been taken.' The man was practically weeping. 'Why didn't the alarm go off and alert the police station?'

One of the two policemen, who had been looking around and closely scrutinising everything as he went, said, 'It looks as if the job's been carried out by someone who knew exactly what they were doing. The alarm system has been disabled. And look —' He pointed to the various CCTV cameras. '— they've been sprayed with paint to stop them recording.'

'I'll have to ring Mr Cavendish,' the shop employee went on, an expression of what looked like dread crossing his face. 'He's going to be appalled. *Appalled*,' he stressed, looking close to tears once more. 'I'm only in charge for a week,' he went on, 'while Mr Hartnell is on holiday. He's back on Monday. Oh God, he'll blame me, say I've been negligent, but I wasn't. I really wasn't ...'

Lexie decided at that point to return to her own salon. She was only in the way here. 'Can I clear up next door?' she asked one of the detectives. 'Nothing's been stolen, after all.'

'Not just yet, love,' he said. 'We need to get the whole area checked, both shops, although I doubt we'll find much in the way of evidence.' He glanced around once more. 'What with all the customers that pass through both places. And the thieves will have been smart enough to have worn gloves for certain.'

Luckily, it didn't take as long as Lexie had expected. More officers arrived; scene of crime officers, she deduced. They closely examined the hole in the wall and the pile of rubble to one side of it before one of them said to Lexie, 'Okay, you can clear up now.' So in the end she'd only had to turn away a dozen or so clients, asking them to come back later when she'd somehow manage to fit them in amongst the other appointments.

Lexie stood looking around. She'd need to get the glass in the door repaired and do something about the hole in the wall, at least temporarily. She hoped her insurance would cover it. The trouble was, she had no sort of burglar alarm, not even the most basic sort, and they might just use that fact as an excuse not to pay. She'd have to see about getting one in light of what had happened. But what was there in here to steal? The hand-held dryers, she supposed, but there was nothing of any real value, and she never ever left any cash in the till.

She was still sweeping up the glass, which seemed to have somehow managed to reach into almost every corner of the salon as well as into the washbasins and beneath the chairs, when her head stylist and best friend, Jordan, came in. She had a later start today because, it being Friday, she worked until eight o'clock. The other stylist, Alice, and the shampoo girl and trainee, Mel, had arrived at their usual times. They were also tidying up between attending to clients, Alice with a great deal of low-voiced grumbling. 'This wasn't in my job description,' Lexie heard at one point as the stylist grudgingly and with exaggerated caution picked glass out of a wash basin. In stark contrast to Alice, Mel was quietly getting on with things. But then, Alice had been trouble almost from the start. So much so, that Lexie was wondering whether to suggest she'd be happier somewhere else, confident that she and Jordan, along with Mel, would cope until they found someone to replace her.

'Oh my God,' Jordan now cried. 'What's happened here?'

Lexie briefly told her, and then showed her the hole in the staffroom wall.

'So nothing's missing? We were just the route into next door?'

'As far as I can see, yes. But next door's lost tens of thousands of pounds' worth by the look of the empty shelves and safe, and judging by the prices in there. Still, they're probably well insured.' Jordan slanted a glance at her. 'Is the man himself in there? Bruno Cavendish? Because I would sure as hell like a good look at him.' She licked her lips lasciviously.

'He's a sight to relish, by all accounts. Handsome, and as rich as Croesus to boot. That's partly due to his shops, but I've heard he has fingers in all sorts of pies: property development, to name just one. He's part of the consortium behind that new out-of-town shopping centre at Halfpenny Fields, and he's apparently made a packet from some very judicious investments.'

'Yeah, well,' Lexie put in, 'all of that means he's so far out of our world, he might as well be on another planet. I mean, have you seen where he lives?'

'Yeah. Adlington Manor. Fab house.'

'It's that, all right.'

Adlington Manor was a large eighteenth-century house, so Lexie had been told. It had originally belonged to the Adlington family. In fact, they'd owned large parts of the town of Adlington at one time — at least, until the end of the nineteenth century. That was when one of the heirs from a fairly long line of dissolute men had finally gambled most of it away. Since then, the land and many of the more substantial properties had been either split up or converted to apartments and then sold off. The house itself had subsequently passed through several different ownerships, until approximately four years ago when Bruno Cavendish had bought it and totally renovated the interior. The exterior, remarkably, had remained in a reasonable condition.

The house could be seen from the road, and Lexie had stopped once to have a good look. No one had been living in it at the time, so, as the gates had been standing open, she'd felt free to go in.

It was three stories high, a rambling construction built of rose-pink brick with a steeply sloping, silver-grey slate roof. This was festooned with a battalion of ornamental chimneys, one for each of the many rooms, she supposed. The windows — she'd counted fifty in all, ranging in size from large to medium, with a few that were so small they could hardly be described as windows at all — were leaded and mullioned, and the entrance was reached via a short flight of steps. A massive oak door flanked with pillars stood at the top of these, and an impressive portico bestowed a look of intimidating grandeur. Surrounding all of this were acres of grounds, unkempt at the time, but perfectly maintained nowadays, she was sure, under the supervision of Bruno Cavendish.

'Shame he lives there all alone,' Jordan went on. 'Well, apart from his five-year-old daughter. His wife left him for someone else two years ago, but he managed to get custody of the little girl. No one has seen her since. I say, do you think he's done her in?' she wickedly concluded.

'I wouldn't think so, no,' she replied. 'I didn't even know his wife had left him or that he'd got custody.' But then, why would she? She'd never been remotely interested in Bruno Cavendish, even though he owned the shop next door. As she'd remarked to Jordan, he inhabited a totally different world to the one they lived in. 'He is divorced, presumably?'

'Well, he certainly behaves as if he is, from all I've heard.'

Lexie raised her eyebrows at her friend and couldn't help grinning. Jordan unashamedly garnered all the local gossip and repeated it to anyone who displayed the slightest interest. In fact, it had become a matter of pride that nothing got past her. 'Oh?'

'Yeah. He's had a string of women ever since. Different one every week, supposedly.'

'You do know what happens to nosy parkers?'

'No. Tell me.'

'They get their very long noses chopped off.'

'Oh, ha-flippin'-ha. There's nothing wrong with being knowledgeable about local affairs.'

'Well, you're certainly that. And it's affairs, literally, by the sound of it in Bruno Cavendish's case.'

'I'd love nothing more than to be on his case.' Jordan gave a loud and raucous laugh.

It was at that point that they were interrupted by a man's voice asking, 'Anyone in there?' It was a smooth, cultured voice, yet at the same time seductively throaty.

They both looked at each other, and Jordan softly asked, 'Could this be the wonderful Mr Cavendish?'

As for Lexie, all she felt was a stabbing of horror. 'Ssh,' she hissed. If it was him, how much of their conversation had he heard? She walked to the doorway of the staffroom and poked her head out. 'Um — yes, I'm here.'

Jordan, of course, couldn't resist following suit. 'We're both here,' she sang.

Lexie closed her eyes in exasperation. How stupid they must look. A pair of heads jutting out, one above the other — Jordan being four or five inches taller than Lexie — through a doorway. Lexie immediately straightened up, bumping Jordan on the chin with the back of her head.

'Ouch,' Jordan grumbled.

But Lexie ignored her. Served her right. And was that a gleam of amusement she could see in the stranger's eye? She wouldn't be surprised. She'd be amused herself if she wasn't so damned embarrassed.

'Hello. I'm Alexis Brookes, Lexie for short.' As she walked towards him, she held her hand out. 'Owner of Clever Cuts.'

Dear God. If this man was Bruno Cavendish — and she was pretty sure he was — he was indeed a sight to behold. For the umpteenth time, Jordan was proved right. It was extremely irritating. Mind you, she conceded, it could also be very useful at times, having the lowdown on someone in advance.

As she'd noticed from her extremely brief sightings of him, he had hair the colour of oiled teak, fairly long and thick, swept back with a single lock falling down onto his forehead. But what she hadn't realised till now was the sheer charisma of the man. He towered over her five feet three inches; she estimated he must be six feet one or two. He was also the possessor of a pair of steely grey eyes; eyes that, at this moment, seemed to be looking straight through her. His nose was very slightly aquiline, and his cheekbones were sharp enough to cut paper. His mouth was well shaped with a full lower lip, and he had the sort of jawline and chin that denoted immense strength of will and determination. Putting it all together, he looked the sort of man Lexie wouldn't want to get on the wrong side of.

He took hold of her hand and said, 'Bruno Cavendish. I own the shop next door.'

'I see.' She chewed at her bottom lip. What a stupid remark. Was that the best she could do? She looked away from the penetrating gaze as she felt her cheeks beginning to warm, which did nothing for either her composure or her confidence. She couldn't believe she still blushed, a blush that steadily deepened as she sensed Bruno Cavendish's gaze moving slowly over her. She was twenty-eight, for heaven's sake. How many other women of twenty-eight still blushed? None that she knew.

She managed to glance back at him, only to discover he was still looking at her, unashamedly taking in her snug sweater and skinny black trousers, before his gaze lifted to linger on her shoulder-length tawny gold hair, her green eyes, her nose and full mouth before returning to her hourglass figure, the curves of which, she was acutely aware, were plainly visible beneath her clothes. It was also plain that he appreciated what he was looking at, because his eyes were gleaming with a disturbing light. Her blush deepened. Even Jordan, she noticed, was staring at her, a quizzical smile tilting her lips.

Belatedly, Lexie realised that Bruno was speaking. Maybe, after all, he hadn't noticed her girly blush.

'Perhaps you'd like to show me the wall that's been damaged,' he said.

Jordan had said nothing throughout this, although probably only a couple of minutes had passed. It just felt longer to Lexie. Lexie glanced at her friend. She was gazing at Bruno, her lips parted, her eyes wide with unmistakable lust. Lexie again nibbled at her lip. She just hoped Bruno hadn't noticed. He'd think they were a right couple of dorks.

'Of course,' Lexie answered, even to her own ears sounding assured and grown up. Confident, in fact. A definite improvement. Even the skin of her face felt cooler, and hopefully it had returned to its normal colour. 'Come this way, would you? It's just in here.' She indicated the doorway that she and Jordan had initially peered out of. 'Did you notice that the glass in the door was broken as well?'

'I did.' His one eyebrow lifted as a gleam of amusement replaced the appreciative warmth, and in a single second Lexie's composure fled. Of course he'd noticed. How could he not have? He'd walked right past the damn thing.

She quickly turned away from him and led him into the staffroom, where she pointed out the hole and the pile of rubble to one side of it. Bruno's glance had narrowed as it swept around; she'd noticed him doing the same in the salon. Clearly, he was missing nothing. His next words confirmed that impression.

'You have no burglar alarm,' he pointed

out. 'Shouldn't you have?' His tone fell miles short of admiring now. In fact, it oozed disapproval.

'Probably.' She hoped she sounded more composed than she felt. She didn't want him knowing how on edge she really was. 'I only took over the salon eighteen months ago and I haven't got round to it. The owner before me hadn't thought it necessary, so ...' She shrugged.

'Pity.' The single word was terse. 'Maybe all this could have been avoided, then.'

She stared at him. There was no mistaking the tone of his voice and what it indicated. He was laying the blame for the burglary squarely at her door because of her lack of security devices. What the hell was he hoping to achieve by doing that? In no way could it be considered her fault.

Stung to her core, Lexie snapped, 'I very much doubt it. According to the two detectives, whoever broke in was an expert. They managed to disable your rather sophisticated alarm system, as well as your CCTV cameras, and then they successfully opened your safe. In which case, they would undoubtedly have disabled any alarm I might have had. And a relatively modest hairdressing salon doesn't justify the sort of security you have. Indeed, I could say that it's the other way round because of all your rather obvious precautions — they do rather advertise the fact that you have plenty worth stealing, wouldn't you say? Your steel shutters, et cetera, et cetera. My salon has been broken into. All your security made it the only feasible way in for them.' *So what do you say to that, Mr Clever Clogs?* she silently added.

He tilted his head to one side and regarded her in silence, eyes still narrowed as they once again scanned her. 'Point taken,' he somewhat grudgingly conceded. 'Okay — I'll get your wall and glass door repaired this morning.'

'Wow!' Jordan exclaimed finally. Lexie had never known her to remain silent for so long. She too must have been overawed by the great Bruno Cavendish. And that was also a first. 'That quickly?'

'Yes.' He smiled then for the first time, and it lifted his looks out of the merely handsome category into something utterly mind-blowing. 'And you are?'

'Jordan Ratcliffe. Hair stylist and chief assistant to Lexie.' Smiling provocatively, she then thrust out a hand towards him, that and her ample breasts. 'We are unisex, so anytime you need a cut and a — blow ...' She literally breathed the word out. He couldn't have missed the sexual innuendo, Lexie decided. 'Dry,' she added, presumably for decency's sake, 'please just come in. I'm sure I'll have no trouble fitting you in.'

Lexie felt her cheeks growing hot again; ferociously hot, in fact, at her friend's outrageous innuendo.

But other than for the most fleeting glint to his eye, Bruno showed no signs of having comprehended Jordan's meaning. He simply smiled and said, 'Thank you. Maybe I'll do that.' He then turned back to Lexie, the smile gone. That really did sting, the fact that he didn't consider her worthy of even the briefest of smiles.

Okay, she didn't possess Jordan's ... assets, but she wasn't that bad. Other men had made no secret of their admiration for her.

'I'll get on with organising those jobs for you,' Bruno added. 'Don't want your customers put off by your state of disrepair.'

'Oh, I'm sure they won't be,' she smoothly responded. 'My customers are very loyal.'

'Good. I'll go and make a couple of phone calls then.'

'That would be greatly appreciated,' Jordan purred. 'Will we be seeing you again soon?'

'I'm sure you will.' He'd kept his gaze on Lexie throughout all of this. 'I'll be back and forth for a few days, restoring order, replacing stock. Nice to meet you both.' He held out a hand. Lexie took it. It was perfectly groomed, smooth and warm. No indications of any manual labour there. Not that that surprised her. She'd doubt he'd ever as much as lifted a trowel, let alone a spade, in his entire life. He'd have minions, she was quite sure, to do such menial tasks for him.

'I'll be seeing you, Ms Brookes,' he said. 'Oh.' He pulled something from the breast pocket of his very expensive-looking jacket. 'Here's my card with my address and phone numbers.'

'Thank you,' she stiffly replied. She briefly glanced at it, and sure enough there was his address, Adlington Manor, as well as a landline and a mobile phone number. 'But I can't imagine that I'll ever need it.' She stuffed it into her trouser pocket.

He regarded her from beneath a lowered brow. She could see he wasn't accustomed to being argued with or treated in such an offhand manner. 'Well, you never know. We are neighbours, after all.' He gave a maddeningly self-assured smile.

'Neighbours? How are we neighbours? You live in Adlington Manor, and I live —'

'I meant here, at the shop.' He raised an eyebrow at her — a sure indication, she decided, of his recognition of her stupidity. Of course he meant the shop. What the hell was the matter with her?

Once again, she felt the infuriating heat of a blush. So it wasn't really very surprising that in the wake of that all she could muster was a weak and rather shaky, 'Of course.'

* * *

But despite what Lexie had labelled as his maddening arrogance, Bruno Cavendish proved to be a man of his word. Just after lunch, a couple of workmen turned up to quickly and efficiently replace the broken glass in the door and repair the brickwork in the wall of the staffroom. They even removed the rubble and swept up the brick dust before applying a thick coating of plaster. 'Let that dry,' one told Lexie, 'and then give it a lick of paint.'

Lexie reflected that whatever his other faults, Bruno Cavendish was clearly a man of his word. But then she supposed that money talks, and as he apparently had shedloads of the stuff — according to Jordan, at any rate — he would speak loudly and very authoritatively indeed.

Business had eventually returned to normal; the clients arrived and were taken care of, even the ones they'd had to turn away earlier, and the rest of the day passed quickly and productively. It wasn't until Lexie was letting herself back into her two-bedroom terraced house that evening that one particular problem raised its head: the problem of Danny and what she was going to do about him. What she was going to do about the two of them, in fact. Because one thing she did know without any doubt: they couldn't go on as they were.

2

Lexie sighed and glanced around as she walked inside the house that she and Danny shared. He clearly hadn't been back, which meant he'd been gone since seven o'clock the previous evening. Mind you, it wouldn't be the first time that he'd stayed out all night, though he usually turned up the next morning full of smooth apologies and equally smooth excuses.

She picked up her phone and pressed the keys for his mobile number. Normally she wouldn't dream of doing this: Danny hated being checked up on, as he saw it; but she was starting to worry now. She couldn't see any indication that he'd been back during the day. She frowned. He'd said he was meeting some friends for a drink and that was all. He hadn't mentioned any names or where he'd be.

When the phone went directly to his

answer service, Lexie felt sufficiently annoyed to leave a terse message: 'Danny, where are you? Ring me when you get this.'

They'd been steadily growing apart over the past few months; so much so that his absences were beginning to outnumber the hours he spent at home with her. The intimacy that had existed between them from their very first meeting two and a half years ago — and which, six months later, had encouraged them to set up home together in this house — had cooled into almost indifference, at least on Danny's part. Which had led Lexie to seriously consider finding her own place. Clever Cuts was doing well, so she could afford it. In fact, she'd even begun to wonder about buying rather than renting, as she and Danny were doing. That was providing she could get a mortgage, of course. But the fact that they were renting meant there should be no difficulty if she left. Yet something — a faint flicker of hope, a reluctance to rush into something she might later regret — had prevented her from taking that step.

If Danny was having an affair, which was something she'd suspected for a while, it would most likely burn itself out, or why hadn't he left her? There must be some vestige of love left, surely? But now, to simply leave — which it was beginning to feel as if he had done, without a word ... well, that was cruel. Needlessly cruel. And she'd begun to wonder whether their time together had meant anything at all to him.

She picked up a photograph of the two of them which she kept on the top of a bookcase, and stared at it. They were having a meal in a local restaurant, and evidently toasting each other with what looked like champagne. She couldn't remember exactly what the occasion was; maybe it was renting this house. It was certainly in the early days of their relationship. She did recall asking the waiter to take the photo.

She gazed at Danny now and sighed. He was a good-looking man, with raven-dark hair and deep, deep blue eyes.

It had been these and the intensity of their gaze that had initially struck her; bowled her over, in fact. They'd first spotted each other in a wine bar. She'd been with a group of friends, while he'd been on his own. He'd made no secret of his admiration of her, openly watching her, making his feelings so obvious that her friends had begun to tease her. It had been Jordan, naturally, who'd beckoned him over, and that had been the start of it all. Lexie had fallen in love almost immediately, as he'd seemed to, and she'd had no compunction about meeting him the following evening. She'd been twenty-five; he'd been twenty-nine. So when he'd suggested living together, she'd immediately agreed. Prior to that, she'd still been living in the house she'd been brought up in. When they'd found this place so quickly, it felt as if it had been meant to happen.

She'd been working at the time as a stylist in another salon. It was where she'd first met Jordan; they'd both joined as trainees ten years previously. Just like her and Danny, they'd developed an instant affinity and had swiftly become friends; a friendship that had intensified into a closeness such as Lexie had never before experienced with another woman, not even with her younger sister, Stella. In fact, so close had they been that they'd been wondering at the time she'd met Danny whether to join forces and rent somewhere. They'd both felt it was time to show some independence and move out of their family homes. Yet Jordan hadn't seemed to mind when Lexie instead announced she was moving in with Danny. 'Go for it, gal,' she'd encouraged her. 'Who am I to stand in the way of true lurve? I just wish I could meet someone too,' she'd wistfully concluded.

It had been Danny who'd first suggested Lexie buy her own salon. She'd been unsure at first — it had felt like a massive step into the unknown — but when her father, who owned two estate agencies, suggested he help her to do it, she'd agreed to go ahead. Once the purchase had gone through, which hadn't taken long — eight weeks in all, it had then seemed a natural progression to ask Jordan to join her as head stylist. 'Is this some sort of compensation for us not moving in together?' Jordan had asked, her tongue stuck very firmly in her cheek. Now, eighteen months later, business was good, and everything would be perfect but for the deterioration of her and Danny's relationship. Yet, strangely, she wasn't feeling as heartbroken as she would have expected, which maybe meant she wasn't as deeply in love as she'd believed.

In the photo he was smiling at her; the smile that, along with his good looks, invariably made women look twice at him. But he'd never seemed to notice, at least not in the beginning. That had begun to subtly change a few months ago, and Lexie had noticed him returning those looks more and more often.

She replaced the frame and sighed again. If only he'd get in touch and offer some sort of explanation. Despite her feelings cooling towards him, she couldn't help but be anxious about him. He could be amazingly irresponsible on occasion. Even so, she couldn't believe he'd simply walk away from her and their life together without a word.

She frowned. What if he'd had some sort of accident and hadn't been able to get in touch with her? She hadn't thought of that. Should she ring his closest friend — the one he almost always said he'd been with if he didn't return home? Brian … damn, what was his surname? She chewed feverishly at her lower lip. Gardener, that was it. But what was his phone number? She had no idea, but there was a very good chance he'd know where Danny was or if something had happened to him. She ignored the fleeting notion that he'd have rung her if there'd been an accident. Unless, of course, he was injured too.

She pulled the phone directory from the bookcase, her heart thumping fiercely. Her fingers shook as she quickly leafed through the pages. She saw that there was only one B. Gardener in Adlington, so she dialled the number. It rang and rang at the other end. Her heart sank. There *had* been some sort of accident. He wasn't at home either. But then, just as she was about to give up, a man's voice said, 'Hello?'

'Brian? Brian Gardener?'

'Yeah, that's me.'

'It's Lexie Brookes, Danny's —'

'Hi, Lexie. How nice to hear from you. How are you? How's Danny? Long time no see.'

Lexie's heart sank for a second time. 'Ah, that's why I'm ringing. I'm a bit worried about Danny. He didn't return home last night.'

'Ho, ho, the dog,' Brian chortled. 'A leopard never changes its spots.' He laughed again.

Those words were the very last that Lexie wanted to hear. She knew from the remarks that some of his friends had made that Danny had had lots of girl-friends prior to her, none of which had lasted longer than a couple of months. In fact, he himself had made no secret of it, even going so far as to brag about this on several occasions. But she'd believed that those days were behind him. Now, she asked herself, had he simply reverted to type? As Brian had just said.

'Um …' She belatedly felt embarrassed. What would he think of her, ringing to ask where her boyfriend was? 'S-sorry to bother you, but I wondered if he —'

'I haven't seen Danny in weeks, Lexie. Sorry.'

'Right. Okay. Thank you.'

'Is he okay?'

'Oh yes,' she lightly answered. 'He's probably just lost track of time. You know Danny, obviously.' She laughed. 'I'm probably being stupid to worry.'

'We-ell, he's always been a bit of a free spirit, but I'm sure you know that. He'll turn up. He always does.'

'Yes, of course he will. Again, I'm sorry to have bothered you.' She quickly ended the call.

So one of his closest friends hadn't seen him in weeks. Which meant Danny had been lying to her when he'd said he'd been with him. In which case, it had to be another woman — otherwise, why lie? So had he, in fact, left her?

She ran upstairs and into the bedroom they shared, and tugged open the wardrobe door. Why hadn't she thought of doing this before, checking his half to make sure everything was still there? She knew there was still a lot belonging to him inside; she'd seen it all that morning when she'd selected her own clothes for the day. Now, she checked each item hanging on the rail. But as far as she could tell, everything was there — apart, obviously, from what he'd been wearing when he'd left yesterday. There were no gaps anywhere. Also, the drawers where he kept his sweaters, et cetera, were full. It was the same in the bathroom; nothing was missing. His toothbrush was there, his aftershave — he'd never have left all of this behind. Which must mean he hadn't deserted her. In which case, that only left an accident. That had to be the explanation. And here she'd been, getting angrier and angrier with him, when he could be lying in a hospital bed seriously injured.

Guilt swamped her; so much so, that she spent the next three quarters of an hour ringing every hospital within a twenty-mile radius, asking if a man named Danny Blake had been admitted. He hadn't.

Finally, she returned to the sitting room and sank down into a chair, her heart lurching with anxiety. She didn't know what else to do, or what to think. All she could do, she finally decided, was wait. Sooner or later he'd have to come home. All he owned was here.

She decided to put an end to the worried speculation — it was achieving nothing — and instead prepare herself something to eat. She'd hardly eaten anything all day, and her stomach was noisily proclaiming that fact. Normally, on a Friday, she and Danny would have eaten out. At the end of the longer working day she was usually exhausted, too exhausted to cook. Now she settled for scrambled eggs on toast, and took her food into the sitting room to sit in front of the television and eat. She needed something other than Danny to occupy her thoughts, but that didn't work. Every sound from the street outside had her leaping up to go and peer through the window, desperately hoping to see Danny out there parking his car and climbing out.

Eventually she tried his mobile number again, but only got the answer service. Yet again she left a message: 'Danny, I'm really worried now. Whatever you might have done, or whoever you're with, ring me. You could at least do that.'

But whatever excuse he had for this extended absence, it had better not involve Brian Gardener. God, how many times had she swallowed his lies? She began to pace the width of the room. And just who was he seeing behind her back? An image floated in front of her then, of Danny in bed with another woman; and despite her anger with him, Lexie's heart ached with misery.

She flopped back down onto the settee. The late-night local news came on the television. The lead item was the break-in at Cavendish Gems. They even showed a shot of the exterior, her salon included.

'. . . the thief or thieves gained entry via the hairdressing salon next door.'

Lexie switched it off. She hadn't noticed anyone with a camera turning up. But then she'd been busy, so why would she? Even as she had the thought, her phone rang. It was her father. He sounded very anxious and worried.

'Lexie, I've just seen the news. Are you okay, love?'

'Yes, Dad. Don't worry, I'm fine.'

'Did they take anything?'

'No, we were just the means of access to next door.'

'It must have been a shock, though. Is Danny there with you?'

'No.'

'No? Where the hell is he? He should be with you.'

'He-he's out, Dad. I'm fine, really.'

And that was the start of it. From then on, the phone rang non-stop, both her mobile and the landline. Everyone she knew — friends, acquaintances, one or two of the clients who hadn't been in that day, the ones she'd given her mobile phone number to — all rang to ask how she was.

Eventually the calls stopped, and she threw herself down onto the settee again. The only person who hadn't called was Danny. Had he not heard what had happened? Probably not. Either that, or he simply didn't care.

Then, as she was heading up the stairs to bed, the phone rang in the hallway. She ran to it and lifted it to her ear. 'Danny?' she cried. 'Is that you?' Although why he'd be ringing the landline, she couldn't imagine.

A man's voice growled, 'No, it isn't. But it's him I want to talk to. He's not answering his mobile phone. So if he's there, put him on.'

'Uh — sorry, who is this?' Lexie demanded. She didn't recognise the voice.

'Never mind who I am,' the man said. 'I want to speak to Danny. I know he's there.'

'No, he isn't. And I don't know when he'll be back. Why do you —' She'd been about to ask why he wanted to speak to Danny when she realised the line had gone dead: the mystery caller had hung up. Lexie stared at the receiver as she replaced it onto its base. Who the hell was that? Was that who Danny had been with? If it was, the man was now seemingly every bit as much in the dark about Danny's whereabouts as she was. But more to the point, why wasn't Danny answering his mobile — not just to her, but to anyone, by the sound of it?

Her heartbeat resumed its frantic thudding. What was happening? Where on earth was he?

3

Lexie spent the better part of that night awake and on the alert for the sound of Danny's key in the front door. It wasn't until the early hours of the morning that she finally drifted into a fitful sleep, which meant she awoke, still exhausted and unbearably tense as she recalled the previous evening's mysterious phone call. Both of these feelings were intensified by a deep unease, because Danny still wasn't back.

She tried his mobile number, but the answering service once again was all she got. She didn't bother leaving a message. What was the point? Despite all the evidence to the contrary, Danny had undoubtedly left her. But why disappear without a word, and without any of his belongings? He must know she'd worry. No matter how much their relationship had deteriorated, she still cared about him, about his well-being. Of course, he'd eventually have to return for his belongings, and hopefully she'd be here when he did — although she wasn't banking on that. If he really had left without saying anything, he'd probably extend that deceit and sneak back while she was at work. But till then, she resolved to get on with her life.

And to reinforce this decision, she muttered, 'Blow you, Danny Blake. I don't need you, so there.'

* * *

'Good God, woman,' was Jordan's initial cry as Lexie walked into the salon. 'Have you had any sleep at all? You look terrible, like a walking corpse.'

'Gee, thanks, Jordan. That's made me feel a hundred percent better.'

'Sorry. Is it all a bit much for you?' She did have the good grace then to look concerned about her friend.

'What?' Lexie frowned at her. She couldn't possibly know that Danny had disappeared.

'The break-in, the damage done, the mind-blowingly sexy Bruno Cavendish.'

It was unfortunate, in the immediate aftermath of that heedless remark, that the door right behind Lexie should open. She swivelled, and to her horror found herself face to face with the man himself. Good grief, did he make it a habit to creep up on people? But more to the point, had he overheard what Jordan had said about him? She slanted a narrowed glance at her friend and saw that Jordan's face was now as red as her own felt. That would teach her to mind what she was saying, Lexie decided.

However, if he had overheard, Bruno Cavendish gave no sign of it. In fact, his expression could best be described as dispassionate; detached, even. Lexie glanced down at the small girl clinging to his hand.

'Hello,' she said with a warm smile. 'And who are you? Have you come in for a haircut? Because we can probably fit you in.' So desperate was she for some sort of distraction for Bruno as well as herself from her friend's remark that she began to gabble, something she had a terrible habit of doing whenever she was nervous or embarrassed. She braved a glance then at Bruno, and to her dismay spotted what couldn't be mistaken for anything other than a knowing glint in his eye as he watched her. Oh God — he had heard, and clearly recognised her tactics for what they were. Now what would he think? That she shared Jordan's opinion of his sexiness? Huh — if only he knew. His high-handed manner of the day before still rankled. He had all but accused her of being negligent in not having some sort of security in the salon, which, in his view, evidently made her at least partially responsible for the break-in and the subsequent loss of all his stock.

'I'm Serena Cavendish. How do you do?' The little girl held out a hand to Lexie. She didn't as much as glance at Jordan. But if she'd heard Jordan's remark, she surely wouldn't have understood it — would she? She was only five years old, for goodness sake — according to Jordan, that was. Lexie once again glanced at her friend, who was now looking positively mortified, which meant she'd also noticed Serena's disregard of her.

Lexie returned her attention to the child. She was small for her age, and with her white-blonde hair and bright blue eyes was ravishingly pretty. Lexie could glimpse nothing of her father in her, so she must owe her looks to her mother, which meant her mother must be a very beautiful woman indeed.

'I'm fine. How are you?' Lexie said. She leaned over and took the proffered hand, then gently shook it.

'I'm fine, too. Thank you for asking,' Serena said. Her manners were impeccable; quaint, even. Lexie was forced to suppress a smile of amusement. 'You know my daddy, I believe?' She indicated her father. His expression, in complete contrast to his daughter's, exhibited no warmth at all, although his eyes had retained their maddening gleam as he regarded Lexie.

'We have met — just yesterday, actually,' Lexie went on. 'Hello, Mr Cav —'

'Oh, please,' Bruno unceremoniously interrupted her, '— it's Bruno. After our shared experience, there's really no need to stand on ceremony.'

Lexie tightened her mouth in exasperation. If that wasn't typical of someone like him. What was it about extremely rich men? Every one that she'd ever encountered — which she had to admit wasn't a great number — had considered himself to have the unquestionable right to disregard what anyone else might have to say, and interrupt whenever they felt like it.

'Shared experience?' she echoed. 'I wasn't aware we'd shared any sort of experience, pleasant or unpleasant.' What the hell was he talking about? It couldn't be the robbery. He hadn't been with her when she'd discovered it, so how could they have shared the experience?

'The break-in. All right, I wasn't actually with you.'

'No, you weren't,' she muttered.

True to form, he carried on as if she hadn't spoken. Again, Lexie felt a stab of exasperation. 'But it must have been a very alarming experience for you to discover it, and then to know your salon had simply been used as a means of getting into my shop.'

'Oh — right. We-ell, yes, it was.'

'So, to make up for it, Serena and I would like to invite you for afternoon tea at the Manor tomorrow afternoon.'

Lexie stared at him, incredulous. Afternoon tea — and at the Manor? Never. Not in a million years. 'Oh, really, th-that's not necessary. It wasn't your fault.'

'Oh, ple-ease come,' Serena put in. 'Daddy said you must have been very frightened, and we really do want to make it up to you. We don't have many visitors, you see.'

Lexie regarded the little girl and the heartfelt plea that was only too visible within her eyes. The poor child was lonely. So lonely that she and her father felt the need to invite a complete stranger to tea. Whatever was Bruno thinking of? They must have friends that they could invite, surely; friends of Serena's own age. Or maybe not, if she didn't attend the local school.

Lexie's heart melted. 'Oh, well . . .' She was torn between an unexpected desire to make this child happy and her reluctance to agree to any sort of concession to the father.

'Please,' Bruno added his plea to Serena's, his gaze warming for the first time since he'd entered the salon. 'And if you have any children, bring them along too. They'd be most welcome.'

'I don't have any children,' she blurted. 'I'm not married.'

He actually grinned at her now, and for a second she was forced to agree with Jordan when she'd described him as mind-blowingly sexy. She took a deep breath. She was not going to fall for it — no way. Good looks weren't everything. In her book, kindness and consideration for others far outweighed that attribute — qualities, she suspected, he sadly lacked.

'That doesn't seem to matter these days,' Bruno said.

'Maybe not to you,' she stiffly retorted, 'but it certainly does to me.'

He quirked an eyebrow at her rebuke. She'd noticed him doing it a couple of times the day before. It must be a particular habit of his; its purpose, she suspected, to demonstrate disdain, maybe disbelief even, of anyone bold enough to disagree with him. Either that, or he considered himself a second Roger Moore.

His subsequently dry words conveyed sarcasm, however, rather than disbelief. 'Well, now that that's been cleared up ...'

She stared at him, not bothering to mask her indignation. He didn't seem to notice. Instead, he looked as if he was struggling to suppress what looked suspiciously like amusement. A sharp stab of irritation pierced Lexie. She glanced down at Serena, who wasn't making any attempt to hide her disappointment at Lexie's lack of any children, before sweeping her gaze back to Bruno. His expression had altered from one of amusement to one of tender concern as he regarded his daughter.

'Even so,' he said, turning back to Lexie, 'we'd still very much like you to come. Please.'

'Yes, ple-ease come,' Serena cried. 'Mrs Wilcox has promised to make her special chocolate cake.'

'Mrs Wilcox?'

'Daddy's housekeeper.'

Of course. How stupid of her. Naturally, he'd have a housekeeper. A divorced man — a hugely wealthy man, according to Jordan, with a small child: he'd hardly take care of her and his domestic responsibilities himself, not with all the business commitments he must have in order to simply maintain his wealth, let alone increase it. Lexie flicked her gaze towards her friend, mutely seeking guidance as to what she should do.

Jordan rolled her eyes at her as if to say, *What the hell are you waiting for? Say yes.*

And really, why didn't she? It would be

a once-in-a-lifetime opportunity to see inside Adlington Manor, because she was sure the chance would never come again. And, of course, that was why Jordan was encouraging her to accept the invitation — so that Lexie could give her graphic details of the furnishings and decor afterwards to add to her fund of local knowledge, and so enhance her reputation for knowing all there was to know about the town and its inhabitants.

Conceding defeat, therefore, she smiled down at the small girl and said, 'Thank you, Serena, I'd be happy to accept your invitation,' placing deliberate emphasis on the word 'your' so that there'd be no doubt about it being Serena's persuasions that had swayed her and not her father's.

The small girl hopped up and down on the spot, gleefully clapping her hands. 'Goody, goody.' She beamed up at her father. 'She's coming, Daddy.'

'So I hear.' He smiled, outwardly at least, with a pleasure that matched his daughter's, before glancing back again at Lexie. 'Thank you. We'll look forward to it. Shall we say four thirty?'

She nodded, panic belatedly setting in at what she'd agreed to. Afternoon tea with the local lothario, no less, that was what. Which sounded utterly ridiculous. She was quite sure his customary style of entertaining a woman would be an intimate meal for two with the champagne extravagantly flowing. She simply couldn't imagine him sipping at a cup of tea. 'Four thirty it is, then.'

'You know where we are?'

'Oh yes, I know where you are.' She smiled grimly. As she was sure the entire female population of Adlington did, certainly any under the age of thirty-five.

Once the pair had left again, it was Jordan's turn to execute a little hop or two of her own. 'You jammy beggar. You're well in there. You could have asked if I could come too.' She gave a much-exaggerated pout.

'Oh, yeah,' Lexie scoffed. 'After your words of a few minutes ago, I wouldn't trust you within inches of him and his house. You'd probably propose.'

'Ah-ha.' Jordan gave a broad grin. 'But propose what?' She then winked, making it clear to Lexie that her proposal definitely wouldn't be one of marriage. 'Seriously though, do you think he heard what I said about him?'

'I'd say he heard all right. I just hope and pray he doesn't assume I share that sentiment about him.'

* * *

The day at the salon was hectic, as Saturday invariably was, with hardly a break for any of the workers. Alice, despite her increasingly sullen moods, got on well, making Lexie wonder whether it would be altogether wise to get rid of her. If only she'd change her attitude towards her employer, Lexie wouldn't even be considering such a step. It was almost as if she was jealous of her boss. The only time Alice smiled and spoke warmly was when Danny put in an appearance, which he had been prone to do a couple of times a week. Then she was chatty and flirtatious, full of giggles. And of course Danny, as he had done more and more of late, responded in kind. Alice would then glow, her cheeks flushing prettily, her eyes shining.

Oh God. Have I been completely blind?

Was it Alice who he'd been seeing? Now that Lexie came to think of it, the woman had seemed genuinely attracted to him. Could he have deserted her too? It would go a long way to explaining Alice's present black mood.

Lexie's mind began to work madly. Could the affair, if that was what it had been, have grown too intense? Had Alice become too demanding? Had Danny grown nervous, afraid that Lexie would find out? Could he have gone to ground somewhere, until the affair cooled? The questions came thick and fast. But the truth was, Lexie wouldn't put it past him to have run away. For all his outward confidence and bluster, Danny could be weak, especially if he lost control of a situation. He'd simply turn his back on it and beat a hasty retreat.

He'd be well aware that if Lexie discovered what he'd been doing, he'd be out of the house and out of her life. And as she paid the larger part of the rent, he wouldn't have a case to argue. He'd always had a habit of flitting restlessly from job to job, telling her each time that this could be the big earner; and then when it wasn't, that the big rewards were just around the corner. But more and more, Lexie had begun to doubt his actual abilities. He grew bored quickly, and wouldn't stick with anything long enough to learn to do the job well. He'd migrated from working on a building site — as the site foreman, he'd said at the time, though she'd later discovered he'd been a brickie — to working in a hardware store: managing it, he'd told her, before moving on to sell insurance. There was a huge monthly bonus to be earned, apparently, if he sold enough; not that Lexie ever saw any evidence of extra money. Danny certainly didn't offer any more towards the rent. And all this had been in the space of a couple of years.

While she'd loved him so deeply, none of it had seemed to really matter; and she'd swiftly dismissed her occasional doubts and concerns, vowing to give him his chance to make good, as he seemed sure he would eventually. To trust him, in other words. But just lately, Lexie hadn't been able to stop herself from questioning his lack of ambition. In fact, she'd begun to ask herself whether he had the ability to stick to anything at all, or to have any sort of successful future. Was she always going to have to support him?

She frowned. Could she perhaps ask Alice if they'd been having an affair? Her answer came even before she'd finished asking herself the question. Certainly not. She had no trouble visualising Alice's triumphant expression as she told her yes, and she wouldn't give the other woman the satisfaction. No way. She'd bide her time and see what happened. Danny would have to return sooner or later, and then Lexie would demand the truth from him. All of it. If he had been having an affair, then whoever it was with, she'd end things between them there and then. She wasn't prepared to play second fiddle to anyone, especially not a member of her own staff.

* * *

By the time she returned home that evening, Lexie was weary but determined. She was going to call a halt to all this worrying about Danny. If he'd left, he'd left. End of story. She didn't need him, not really. She had a thriving and profitable hairdressing business. But more than that, she wasn't even sure that she loved him any longer. Oh, she was fond of him, and he could be great company when he was in the right mood. But could she imagine spending the rest of her life with him? That was something she was no longer confident about.

She prepared herself a meal, poured herself a large glass of red wine, and sat down in front of the television. Although it was dark, being the end of September, she hadn't yet drawn the curtains. She liked to see the passing beams of car headlights and the sight of people walking past the window, especially now she was alone.

It wasn't until the programme she was watching was over and she noticed it was ten o'clock that she stood up and went to the window, intending to pull the curtains across and finally shut the night out. She glanced up and down the road, wondering if she'd see Danny, but she didn't. What she did see was a figure standing on the opposite pavement, motionless, in the shadow of one of the large trees that punctuated the roadside at regular intervals.

She stared hard. It was a man; he just wasn't Danny. In fact, he was considerably more heavily built than Danny, and quite a bit taller; three or four inches at least. But who was he, and why was he skulking under a tree?

A couple of minutes went by and he didn't move. In fact, Lexie got the distinct impression that he was watching her, or at least watching the house. A trickle of unease quivered through her then, as she recalled the phone call of the evening before. Could it be the same man, waiting for Danny? Could he be watching her; watching the house?

She tugged the curtains across, and a moment later the landline rang. She jumped, every nerve ending leaping, and went into the hallway where the cordless phone sat on its base. She stared at it for a moment before lifting it slowly to her ear.

'Yes?'

'Is he there?' the gravelly tone demanded. 'I want to speak to him.'

'I-If you mean Danny, then no he isn't, and I don't know where he is. Why do you —'

But just as it had last time, the line went dead. Lexie immediately tapped out 1471 for the caller's number, but the automated voice told her that there was no number to return the call.

With a hand that trembled, she replaced the phone, before returning to the sitting room and going directly to the window. She swept the curtain to one side and peered out.

There was no one there. The street was quite empty.

4

Yet again Lexie tried Danny's number, and yet again she was transferred to an answering service. Exasperated almost beyond endurance, she threw her mobile down onto the settee before walking into the kitchen and pouring herself another large glass of wine. What the hell was he playing at?

'Whatever you've done and wherever you are, Danny, I hope you're pleased with yourself,' she muttered. 'Not only have you seriously upset me, but you've also upset a very sinister-sounding man.'

And with that she downed the entire glass of wine in one go, after which, in a mood of utter defiance, she poured herself another.

* * *

It wasn't that much of a surprise when she crawled out of bed the next morning to feel her head hammering and her stomach churning. It was no more than she deserved. She'd downed a whole bottle of wine, after all.

Lexie clutched at her forehead, rubbing at it, kneading her temples, as she tried to ease the painful throbbing. What the hell had she been thinking of? Huh! Stupid question. She knew what she'd been thinking of — or rather who she'd been thinking of. Danny. No matter how hard she tried, she hadn't been able to drive him from her thoughts. But it hadn't just been Danny. She'd mentally replayed the two mysterious phone calls over and over, asking herself who the man could possibly be. More than that, though — much more, was the threat that she was beginning to sense emanating from him. But that was no excuse. No matter how troubled she was, she never ever drank that much; she hadn't the head for it.

She smiled grimly to herself and pulled

on her dressing gown. Thank the Lord it was Sunday and she didn't have to go to work. Coffee, she needed coffee. That would get her going.

She was downstairs and filling the kettle before she remembered. Sunday. And she was expected for tea at Adlington Manor. She gave a heartfelt groan. In that second, given a choice, she'd happily opt for death and the chance to lie in a coffin, with its lid closed, shutting out the world and all its problems. Yes, even that, rather than being compelled to sit and make polite conversation with Bruno Cavendish.

Hang on, though — she could ring and cancel. Of course she could. She didn't have to go. She could plead sickness — which wasn't a lie, because she did feel sick; extremely sick. And she had both his phone numbers. She'd even entered his mobile number into her speed dial. Why, she didn't know. It was highly unlikely she'd ever need to ring him — till now, that was.

But even as her finger hovered over

the key, an image of the plea in Serena Cavendish's eyes appeared before her, and she knew she didn't have it in her to disappoint the little girl. It wasn't her fault that her father was such an obnoxious, cocky individual.

With that, her nausea intensified; and, knowing she wouldn't make it upstairs to the bathroom in time, she leant over the sink, where she energetically threw up. After which, she did feel fractionally better.

Three cups of black coffee and two slices of toast later, she was practically back to normal. She showered and dressed in her favourite jeggings and baggy sweater. Then, to ensure a total recovery, she poured herself a fourth cup of coffee. Once she'd drunk it she pulled on a warm jacket, desperate all of a sudden to escape the house and its memories of Danny and happier times. She'd have a walk on the nearby common. It was only just after one o'clock, and as it was a perfect end-of-September afternoon, she didn't want to spend it indoors. And she didn't need to set out for Adlington Manor until four fifteen at the earliest.

As Lexie closed the front door behind her, she glanced upwards. The sun blazed down from a speedwell-blue sky, its perfection only marred by the odd puffball cloud. It was also warmer than she'd expected, so unzipping her jacket, she strode out briskly and began climbing the hill that would take her onto the common. Several other people had all evidently had the same idea. To a man and woman, they smiled as they passed, each of them looking enviably carefree.

In a bid to empty her mind of any further thoughts of Danny and the mystery man, Lexie walked and walked, until she'd left everyone else behind. Ahead of her, she spotted a copse of trees; well, a small wood, actually. She could see a path threading through it, and as she'd never been this far before, she decided to indulge in a spot of exploring. She strode into its partial shade, admiring the lacework of sunlight and shadow that dappled the ground in front of her as she did so. A dog barked somewhere, and a lone robin sang from a branch in a golden-leafed beech tree. She breathed deeply. The air smelt of the pine needles she was treading underfoot, and woodsmoke. Someone, somewhere, must have a bonfire going. She took another deep breath and sighed it back out, then repeated it twice more. This was exactly what she needed: fresh air, deep breathing, and something else to think about.

A branch cracked behind her as if someone had trodden on it. Surprised, she stopped walking and glanced back. She'd believed she was alone. She looked around, but couldn't see anyone. Yet for all that, she had the sense that someone was there, somewhere in the shadows beneath the trees. Lexie peered into the depths of the wood, seeking out a bulky, tall figure. She thought she detected a movement, but the harder she peered the less she could make out, mainly due to the darkness being cast by the dense foliage of the tree canopy.

She swivelled around again and

lengthened her stride before making a sharp left turn, following a narrower pathway; one that she could see ultimately led to a patch of ground that was a great deal lighter than the one she was in at the moment. If her sense of direction was accurate, it should lead her out from beneath the tree cover and back into the open ground. Before that, however, it was as if she was still walking in semi-darkness. In fact, she could have done with a torch. Her step slowed, due to the brambles that carpeted the ground. They lay so thickly that she lost sight of the pathway. Indeed, with every step she took the prickly tendrils wrapped themselves round her ankles, clinging to her jeggings and threatening to trip her up.

Her heart began to hammer as, for the second time, she thought she heard footsteps behind her. Desperate now to reach the sunlight that she could see ahead of her, she broke into a sort of a jog — not easy, considering the density of the undergrowth all around her. Low-hanging tree branches snagged in her hair, and tendrils of the gorse which interspersed the brambles tugged at her. It all conspired to seriously slow her down. And all the while, her senses screamed at her to move faster; to get away. To run.

Finally, panting heavily, Lexie managed to escape from the shadows and erupted back into the sunlight. She spotted a couple with a dog walking just ahead of her. She'd stay close to them. She darted another swift glance behind her, and it was then that she made out the figure of a man standing motionless beneath the trees. The same man who'd been outside in the street the evening before.

It couldn't be denied any longer. She was being watched; followed now as well. Was he expecting her to meet up with Danny? She couldn't think of any other explanation for this . . . this stalking.

She broke into a fast jog then, keen to get off the common where she was feeling way too vulnerable. Within fifteen minutes was letting herself back into the house, by which time her chest was heaving — as much with fear as from her exertions. Heaving so hard, in fact, that she could barely draw a breath. She bent double, resting both hands on her knees as she fought for calm, at the same time asking herself a couple of questions.

The first was, could she be in danger from this man? Danny had clearly upset someone seriously enough to make whoever it was stake out her home. The man must have reasoned that she was his only means of finding Danny.

The next question was, what would he do if Danny didn't return home? And the answer to that was something she didn't dare consider.

But she did have one answer, at least. The reason for Danny's disappearance was not because he'd left Lexie for another woman, but because he was frightened to return home and face this man.

Once she'd caught her breath again, Lexie changed out of her walking clothes into a black above-the-knee skirt and matching opaque black tights. She teamed them with a pale green lightweight jumper. She then regarded her reflection in the full length mirror, her gaze a keen one as she turned this way and that. Was the skirt too short, the jumper too tight? It hugged her breasts, boldly emphasising their full curves. She recalled the manner in which Bruno's gaze had moved over her at their first meeting, his appreciation of what he was looking at barely concealed. Would the same thing happen this time?

Lexie nibbled at her bottom lip as she continued to inspect her reflection. The last thing she desired was for him to think she was deliberately inviting his scrutiny; in other words, making a play for him. She was sure he was conceited enough to presume such a thing. His sense of self-worth was considerable; that had been all too evident during their brief encounters. She frowned, still staring in the mirror. The trouble was, all of her sweaters were the same. Oh, to hell with it. He could think what he wanted. She really didn't care. And after this afternoon, she need never see him again.

She slipped on a dark green jacket and

black ankle boots to complete the outfit. She then wound a silky scarf around her neck and let it trail down over her front, effectively disguising her curves. With that done, she looked back into the mirror, and belatedly realised her hair was a complete mess: tousled, all over the place, the inevitable result of her mad dash through the trees. She sighed. What was wrong with her? Normally she would have tidied her hair and applied her makeup before dressing. Another consequence of her frightening experience on the common? Either that, or the equally frightening prospect of tea with Bruno Cavendish. Whichever it was, her nerves were well and truly shredded.

She removed her jacket and the scarf and attempted to repair the damage to her hair. The shoulder-length bob was supposed to be sleek and smooth, but that look had gone out the door, and now it proved almost impossible to exert any control at all over the dishevelled strands, no matter how hard she attacked them with her brush. They stubbornly insisted on going every which way. In the end, in desperation, she resorted to piling them all into a spiky heap on the top of her head and firmly anchoring them with pins, before spraying a lot of lacquer over it all, praying that it would stay in place. It wasn't the effect she'd wanted, and it hardly reflected her skills as a stylist, but it would have to do. She hadn't got time to shampoo and blow dry it, which was what it really needed. She applied a light cover of makeup, streaked some pale green shadow on her eyelids, brushed mascara onto her lashes, and finished off with a rose-pink lipstick. A spray of her favourite perfume completed the less-than-perfect job, and she was ready. She cocked her head at the mirror. Well, more or less. She then put the jacket and scarf back on.

Adlington Manor was just that bit too far for her to walk to it, especially after her scare earlier. And it would most likely be starting to get dark by the time she left again anyway. Lexie picked up her car keys and went out to where she'd parked her Polo just a short distance along the road. She climbed in and started the engine, then realised she'd got nothing to take for Serena as a hostess gift. So she decided to stop at the garage on the way, looking for something suitable for a five-year-old girl. However, that was easier thought of than accomplished, and she was forced to make do with a couple of packets of sweets and a colouring book, all of which seemed very boring and extremely unimaginative.

Five minutes later, she was driving between high wrought-iron gates and along the driveway that led to the house. Although she'd already seen it close up, it now looked even more intimidating than before, mainly because it had been uninhabited, she guessed.

She climbed from the car and mounted the steps to the front door. She'd just raised her hand to ring the bell when it sprang open, and Bruno and a beaming Serena stood there.

'You came!' the little girl cried.

'Of course.' Lexie smiled at her. 'I

always keep my promises. I've brought this for you.' She proffered the sweets and the book.

'Oh, thank you,' Serena said. 'But really you shouldn't have bothered.' Clearly, she wasn't any more impressed with the gift than Lexie had been.

Bruno murmured, 'Five going on fifteen — wouldn't you agree?' Then he grinned at her before saying, 'No present for me? How disappointing.' And his eyes glittered provocatively at her.

Lexie felt the hated tide of colour begin to rise up her face. She gnawed at her lip. When was she ever going to grow out of this infuriating habit? 'Sorry,' she muttered, 'but I didn't think you'd appreciate sweets or a colouring book.'

'Touché,' he murmured. 'Actually, just your presence here is gift enough for me. Thank you for coming.' He reached out and took hold of her hand, then lifted it to his lips and gently dropped a kiss upon it.

As she had no answer to either his words or the unexpected gallantry of the gesture, Lexie remained silent, and she managed to avoid Bruno's gleaming gaze as he raised his head again. She had a very strong suspicion that he was relishing teasing her and thoroughly enjoying the sight of her rosy cheeks. She tightened her mouth, reflecting that such behaviour didn't bode well for the next hour or so. Not surprisingly, she found herself wondering how soon she could leave again without appearing rude.

'Please, come in.' He moved to one side, drawing his daughter with him, allowing Lexie to enter the house.

She found herself in the sort of hallway typical of a stately home. It was bigger than the entire ground floor of her house, which admittedly wasn't large, comprising only a modestly sized breakfast kitchen and a sitting room. The hallway was little more than postage-stamp size. This hall, however, was a huge expanse of marbled apricot-and-cream tiles. It contained several heavily carved high-backed chairs sitting against the walls, an oak settle, and something which Lexie believed was called a coffer; it was a large carved box. There were three extremely ornate side tables upon which various objets d'art were artistically displayed, and in the very centre of the floor there was a round pedestal table on which was the largest bowl of bronze-and-cream chrysanthemums that she'd ever seen. There was an inglenook fireplace which, instead of a fire, contained a huge colourful arrangement of autumn foliage. There were several heavily framed oil portraits on the walls, as well as a couple of impressive busts on plinths. Lexie wondered if the portraits depicted some of Bruno's ancestors. A broad flight of stairs led up to the bedrooms, presumably.

Bruno had clearly noticed her looking at the portraits, because he said, 'Not my family, I'm afraid. I have no one so grand. I bought them with the house; the seller didn't want them — well, had no room for them, he said. I decided the walls would look too bare without them, so I left them there. Now, let me take your coat.'

Lexie removed her jacket and handed it

to him. With all this grandeur surrounding her, she wouldn't have been at all surprised if a butler had appeared to perform that duty. But instead, Bruno handed it to Serena, who then ran to a door that Lexie guessed led into a cloakroom.

'Okay. Now we're having tea in the snug,' Bruno told her. 'It's a great deal cosier than the large drawing room, and it's where Serena and I mostly spend our time together.' He ushered her into a room that despite its description as snug was still twice the size of her sitting room. Deeply cushioned cream upholstered armchairs and settees formed a semicircle on a pale green carpet. Opposite them was a large flat-screened television along with a satellite box and a DVD player; these sat to the side of a second inglenook fireplace, a smaller one this time than the one in the hall, with a pile of logs that was ready to light. On the other side of this was a set of shelves that reached almost to the ceiling. They mostly held books, but a couple of the lower ones were devoted to what looked like boxes of games. A low table was set in the midst of the armchairs and settees, laden with plates of sandwiches and fruit tartlets, as well as three sorts of cake. Lexie instantly noticed the fabled chocolate cake, and it did look absolutely delicious. There was a teapot and all the trappings that went with it.

Serena ran back in and positioned herself on one of the two settees. She was so petite that it dwarfed her. She patted the cushion next to her and said to Lexie, 'You sit by me.'

Lexie hid a smile. Clearly she'd inherited her father's authoritarian tendencies, but nevertheless she did as she was instructed. It was certainly a whole lot better than having to sit alongside Bruno on the other settee. But when he seated himself in a chair almost immediately opposite them, she wasn't sure that that wasn't worse, because he was now in a position to observe every move she made.

5

And it didn't take him long to do exactly that. Just as Lexie had feared, his gaze roamed over her hastily arranged hair and her full pink lips, before moving down to the clinging sweater and the skirt that had by this time ridden halfway up her thighs. No wonder he was staring.

'You look very nice,' he eventually said.

For the second time — or, she wondered, was it the third? — the warmth crept up her face, and a quiver of amusement quirked the corners of Bruno's mouth as she haltingly replied, 'Th-thank you.' After which, she made a hopefully unobtrusive but sadly abortive effort to pull the skirt down, at the same time struggling to conceal her embarrassment. She couldn't understand it. She didn't normally feel this uncomfortable with a man; any man, in fact. The trouble was, this particular man seemed to have the knack of somehow laying bare every one of her uncertainties and vulnerabilities, all without actually saying very much. It was quite, quite maddening. Especially when she really didn't care a jot what he thought of her.

Mind you, in her favour it had to be said that she wasn't accustomed to receiving compliments. Danny had rarely made the effort in all the time they'd been together. She could probably count his complimentary remarks on the fingers of one hand and still have at least a couple left untouched. In fact, in recent months she'd begun to wonder whether he even saw her properly anymore. The sort of admiration she was being subjected to by Bruno Cavendish had therefore caught her well and truly on the back foot.

'I hope you're hungry,' he said, indicating the sumptuous spread in front of them. 'But first, how about a cup of tea?'

'Yes, please,' she instantly answered. Her throat was drier than the Gobi desert; and that, she was sure, was down to nervous tension. Again, all Bruno's fault.

'Milk and sugar?'

'Just milk, please, and only a dash of that.'

He proceeded to deftly wield the milk jug and teapot, and placed a cup and saucer of steaming liquid in front of her.

Lexie was surprised. She hadn't expected him to pour the tea. She'd assumed the housekeeper would appear to do the honours.

He slanted a glance at her. 'You look surprised. Did you think I wouldn't be capable of pouring some tea?'

'Oh, n-no; no.'

'Liar,' he murmured, filling his own cup as he did so. He then handed Serena a glass of milk.

'Thank you, Daddy.'

'Pass Lexie the sandwiches, sweetheart.'

The little girl leaped to her feet, placing her glass on the table before expertly picking up a tea plate, a serviette, and finally a plate of beautifully cut and arranged sandwiches, making Lexie wonder how many times she'd done this before. Did Bruno make a habit of inviting women to tea? It seemed very out of character if he did.

'There are egg and cress, smoked salmon and cream cheese, and tuna and mayo,' Serena solemnly told Lexie.

'All my favourites,' Lexie said.

The girl beamed her delight and giggled. 'Have one of each, then.'

'Well, I don't know about that,' Lexie answered. 'I have to watch my figure.'

'Why?' Bruno bluntly asked. 'It looks pretty good to me; perfect, in fact,' he concluded in a throaty voice, as he once again slid his gaze over her.

'Thank you, Serena.' Lexie pointedly ignored her host's extremely and deliberately, she suspected, provocative remark. 'You're very good at this. Do you host tea parties very often?'

'Quite often,' Serena told her, 'when Daddy invites someone.'

She sensed Bruno's gaze still on her, and she couldn't resist returning it — an action she instantly regretted, because what she encountered was knowing amusement. Damn; damn. He believed she was deliberately probing Serena to find out more about him, and that had been the last thing she'd intended. She had absolutely no interest in his social engagements or how many women he invited to his home. However, he thought otherwise, as his next remark revealed.

'She means our relatives. Quite often elderly aunts.'

'And Granny and Grandpa,' Serena corrected him. 'Oh, and Auntie Pattie and Uncle Lucas.'

'My brother and sister,' Bruno put in. 'Not that they come often. Much too busy with their social lives,' he drily concluded.

'Do they have families?' Lexie asked.

'No, I'm the only one with that pleasure. They're resolutely single, I'm afraid. And of course, as you probably know, I'm single again too — at the moment.'

At the moment? Was he thinking of remarrying then?

'I'd really like some cousins,' Serena sadly said, 'to play with.'

'Don't you have any friends to spend time with? To have sleepovers with?'

'What's sleepovers?'

'Well, you have friends to spend the night with you.'

'Oh, I see. No. I don't know many children.'

Lexie felt a piercing of pity for the little girl.

'She's just started school at Winter House,' Bruno said. 'She hasn't really made any friends yet.'

Winter House was a very exclusive private school that took children from the age of four up to eleven, after which they moved on to somewhere else. To another equally exclusive private school, probably. Lexie doubted whether many of its pupils would live locally. She'd heard they came from miles around to attend, so good was its reputation. They could even board if they wished.

Serena pulled a face at Lexie. 'I don't like any of them, that's why. They tease me — especially Felicity Green. She's horrid.'

'Well, I'm sure you'll get to know them. You'll have to be patient. It takes time to make friends.'

'That's what I've told her,' Bruno said. 'It's her birthday in a while —'

'Not for seven months, Daddy,' Serena promptly corrected him.

'— and we'll have a party and invite them all,' Bruno concluded.

Serena sighed. 'They won't come.'

'Well, how about I invite Lexie to have a day out with us?' he patiently went on — slightly desperately, it had to be said.

Lexie almost felt sorry for him. It must be difficult being a single father trying to cope with a small but very determined girl. She wondered where her mother was. Did she ever visit her daughter? She'd have to ask Jordan. For sure, she'd know. Lexie smiled to herself. After all, there wasn't much she didn't know about Adlington's inhabitants.

'Oh, yes,' Serena cried. 'That would be wonderful.'

Lexie gave a weak smile. She hadn't banked on another invitation. She'd been positive that this would be the one and only; had counted on it, in fact. So — now what?

'Would you, Lexie?' Serena asked. 'We could go to the zoo.'

'We-ell ...' Lexie floundered, desperately searching for a plausible excuse, and failing miserably to come up with a single one.

'Ple-ease,' the little girl beseeched her.

'Serena, don't pressure Lexie.' Bruno's intervention was unexpected, as was the expression on his face. It was every bit as beseeching as his daughter's. 'She might not have the time.'

'It would have to be on a Sunday again,' Lexie said, helpless against the pair of them.

'Goodie.' Serena clapped her hands.

'Are you sure?' Bruno anxiously asked, for all the world as if he hadn't engineered this, which Lexie was quite sure he had. What his motives were for wanting to include her in their lives, she couldn't imagine. They were about as much alike as the moon and the sun — he and Serena in their world of wealth and luxury, she in hers of hard work and not very much money, and therefore destined to never, ever get together.

However, despite her troubling afterthoughts as she wondered what the hell she was letting herself in for, Lexie nodded and took a large bite of her egg and cress sandwich, only to swallow it the wrong way and begin to choke.

Serena leaped to her feet and began to bang her hard on her back.

'Steady on, darling,' Bruno cautioned. 'You don't want to snap Lexie's spine.'

But Lexie managed to regain control and huskily said, 'I'm okay now, thank you.'

Bruno relaxed back into his chair, holding his cup and saucer and taking the occasional sip of tea, as if he did it all the time — which, for all Lexie knew, he might do. Though she was pretty certain his usual tipple would be an alcoholic drink. Champagne, probably, as she'd already decided once before.

'So, tell me,' he drawled, 'how long

have you had your own salon?'

'Eighteen months. The previous owner was keen to retire and let me have it for a good price and a quick sale.'

'And is it doing well?'

'At the moment, yes.'

'So, your friend, uh ...'

'Jordan.'

'Jordan — she works with you?'

'Yes. I have one other stylist as well, and a trainee.'

'Good for you.' He cocked his head and studied her. 'You're very young to have your own business.'

'I'm twenty-eight. That's not so young.' She added, 'How old are you? Not much more, I would guess.'

'Thirty-five,' he murmured.

'Thirty-five. Just seven years older, and yet you have numerous business interests, I believe.'

He took another mouthful of tea, not removing his gaze from her while he did so. 'That's right. But seven years can make quite a difference in one's lifetime.'

He paused, heavy lids shuttering his

expression from her, making her wonder what was coming next. She didn't think she'd ever met anyone quite like Bruno Cavendish before. For the fact was, she didn't know from one moment to the next what he was going to do or say. It was unnerving.

She wasn't left wondering for long, however, because he bluntly asked, 'Is there a husband, or maybe partner in your life?' After which, he made a point of glancing at her ringless left hand.

'A partner. Danny Blake. But … I'm not sure.' She stopped talking abruptly, causing his one eyebrow to lift. She'd belatedly realised she had no desire to discuss her private life and its current problems with this man. She'd only known him for a very short time, after all.

'You're not sure?' His expression sharpened.

Damn. She should have known he'd pick up on her hesitation. She was beginning to realise he was far too perceptive for comfort; in particular, her comfort. What must it be like to live with him?

You'd have no secrets from him, that was for sure. Maybe that was why his wife had left — who'd want their every word picked apart?

'No,' Lexie answered his question. Then, to her complete disgust, she heard herself saying, 'He seems to have gone walkabout at the moment.' What was the matter with her? She'd had no intention of telling him that.

Bruno frowned. 'Does he make a habit of doing that?'

'Of late, yes.' She bit at her lip. There she went again. Why was she sharing these things with someone who was little more than a stranger?

The eyebrow lifted even higher. She stared at it. Any higher and it would disappear beyond his hairline.

'And you put up with that?'

She shrugged. She'd said more than enough. What she put up with, and from whom, was none of his business.

'Daddy,' Serena cut in, 'stop questioning Lexie. Lexie, have some cake.'

Lexie did, and the conversation

reverted to the commonplace once again. It wasn't until much later that she realised Bruno had told her nothing at all about himself.

They arranged to visit the zoo on the following Sunday, and as an hour and a half had gone by since she'd arrived, Lexie got to her feet and said, 'Well, it's been a real pleasure, Serena, but I do have to go.'

'Oh no.' The little girl pouted. 'Why?'

'Serena,' Bruno intervened, 'Lexie has said she's got to go, and that's that.' He swung back to Lexie. 'I'll see you out.'

Serena slumped back into the corner of the settee, still pouting, her arms crossed in front of her, as one foot kicked back and forth on the settee base, setting up a loud drumming sound.

'Sorry about that,' Bruno murmured once they were in the hallway and he'd fetched Lexie's jacket. 'She's lonely, I'm afraid.'

'I could see that. Do no other children live nearby that you could ask here for her?'

'If there are any, I don't know about

them. We're situated pretty well on our own here. No neighbours, as I'm sure you noticed. Anyway, thank you for coming. It was very kind of you to take pity on us.'

He smiled at her, and took her breath away completely. This man was dangerous, too attractive by half. And what had she done? She'd only gone and agreed to meet him and Serena again. Lexie sighed. So much for her conviction that she'd never have to see him again after today.

'So we'll see you next Sunday,' he said. 'I'll pick you up at midday. We'll have lunch somewhere and then go on to the zoo. Hopefully it won't be too tedious for you that way.'

'Um …'

'Yes?'

The tone of his voice, as well as the darkening of his expression, told Lexie that he knew what she was going to do, as surely as he knew night followed day. She was going to make an excuse; recall a reason why she couldn't go with them. She already had her mouth open to say sorry but she'd forgotten she was meeting

Jordan, when, completely out of the blue, she knew she couldn't disappoint Serena. She couldn't punish the little girl just because she herself couldn't bear to spend any more time with Bruno. And it was then that she had a brainwave.

'Actually,' she went on, 'I've got a friend who has a little girl about the same age as Serena. Shall I ask her to join us? I'm sure my friend would appreciate some time to herself.'

'Would you do that?'

He seemed astonished and more than a little relieved at her offer. Maybe it wasn't only Serena who was lonely. Yet why would a man as handsome and wealthy as Bruno be lonely? He must have women practically falling over him for the chance to get to know him.

'Of course,' Lexie told him.

'That would be marvellous. Thank you.'

'You're welcome.' She swung away, slipping her arms into the jacket he was holding out for her.

'Lexie?'

'Yes?' She swivelled back to him and

discovered him much closer than she'd expected — too close; their faces were only a couple of inches apart. Her heart lurched at the same moment as the breath snagged in her throat. She gave a small gasp.

'It's been a real pleasure.' He moved his head the required two inches to allow his lips to lightly brush hers. 'Thank you,' he whispered.

As his breath feathered the skin of her face, Lexie's heart once more leaped in her breast, and her pulse went haywire. She froze, allowing Bruno the opportunity to slide his arms around her and pull her close. The kiss that had been lightly casual till then deepened into something else entirely; and before she knew it he was pulling her even closer, flattening her breasts against his chest, and she was parting her lips as he ground his mouth over hers, passionately and ardently.

'Daddy? Lexie?'

They sprang apart, both breathing fast and deep.

'I want to kiss Lexie goodbye too.'

Oh God was all Lexie could think. Serena had seen them. Somehow she managed to slow her breathing and regain control of her heartbeat. She held her arms wide for Serena to run into, then lifted her up. The little girl weighed almost nothing; it was like holding a doll. Serena entwined her arms around Lexie's neck and whispered, 'I love you, Lexie.'

'I love you too, darling,' she murmured back. And it wasn't a lie. She felt a great tenderness for the little girl. 'I'll see you next Sunday, and maybe I'll have a surprise for you.' She set Serena back on the floor and lifted her gaze to Bruno's. Passion still smouldered, and again she felt her pulse quicken as her heartbeat followed suit.

'Bye, then,' she said, desperate to escape the disturbing intensity of his gaze. It moved over her face, inch by inch, searching — for what? The last thing she wanted was for him to detect how deeply she'd been affected by his kiss.

For the truth was that if he went on behaving like this, there was a very real danger she'd fall in love with him — and that could only lead to pain and heartache for her. For she'd already concluded that she and Bruno Cavendish weren't just worlds apart; they were an entire universe apart.

6

As Lexie drove home, all she could think about was the feel of Bruno's mouth on hers, and the intense physical arousal that it had induced within her. It had been a long time since she'd experienced anything so powerful. But even so, what the hell had she been thinking, responding the way she had? And, more importantly, what must Bruno be thinking? Most likely that she was cheap and easy. After all, she'd practically fallen into his arms.

She groaned at the prospect of having to face him the following Sunday. Would he expect to kiss her again? Knowing him as she was starting to, she wouldn't be surprised, especially as she'd made no attempt to stop him. If Serena hadn't interrupted them ... She gave an even deeper groan. What the hell had she started? And it wasn't as if there was a realistic possibility of any sort of long-term relationship between them. He would always be in his realm of wealth and power, and she'd be lagging miles behind with neither.

However, all that was driven from her head once she arrived home. She was hanging her jacket in the cupboard in the hallway when something distracted her. She sniffed. What was that smell? Cheap aftershave? Had someone been in here?

She strode into the sitting room and looked around. There was no one there. She went into the kitchen. Again, no one. She listened for a moment, and then she ran up the stairs and into her bedroom. That too was empty. Yet the smell was everywhere. She frowned.

Had Danny been home? But he didn't wear cheap aftershave. He'd always sworn he'd rather wear nothing than that. Still, that could have changed. Could he have been back to collect his things?

She went to the wardrobe and tugged the door open. If his clothes had gone ... But they were all there, hanging alongside hers. A quick rifle through told her that nothing was missing. Could she have been burgled? She went to the dressing table and opened the top drawer where she kept all her jewellery. That too was all there. So it wasn't a burglary. Not that her jewellery was worth very much. Well, except for her mother's engagement ring, which her father had given her in the wake of her mother's death.

She went back downstairs to the sitting room. The television set was in its customary place, and her laptop was lying on the settee right where she'd left it. Any sort of burglar would have taken that, surely.

Lexie stood still, her thoughts churning as a single question hammered at her. The man who'd been watching her, who'd followed her earlier; the man who'd phoned, asking for Danny — could it have been him? And if it had been, had he been searching for something; something he believed Danny had? But what? Had Danny stolen something of his? Yet nothing had been moved, and if he'd been searching the place, surely it would have been — unless he didn't want Lexie to know he'd been in here. And, let's face it, but for the smell of the aftershave, she would have had no idea. But if he had been inside, how had he got in? There was no evidence of a break-in. Could he have somehow managed to get hold of Danny's key?

Lexie's heartbeat stilled. Did that mean he'd hurt Danny? There was no other way he could have gained possession of the key. Or was she imagining things?

Maybe she should call the police. But what would she say? She had a feeling that someone had been inside her home, but hey, nothing had been stolen. They'd laugh at her.

She poured herself a glass of wine. At this rate, she was in serious danger of becoming an alcoholic, but the truth was she needed a drink.

She switched on the television and sat down, making every effort to concentrate on the programme; to forget that someone might have let himself in and rifled through her and Danny's belongings. But it was to no avail, and in the end she gave up and went to bed.

But there was no reprieve to be had even there. She had deeply disturbing dreams: one minute she was making love with Bruno, the next she was being pursued through the trees again by a man with Bruno's face.

Which meant that come the next morning, she felt drained and exhausted. She dragged herself from bed, once again with a thumping headache from downing the best part of a bottle of red wine. She had to stop this. She wouldn't find the answers she sought that way.

* * *

For a second time, Lexie arrived at the salon to be greeted by Jordan's cry of, 'Oh no, did the tea party go badly?'

'What?' Lexie frowned at her.

'Tea party — did it go badly?'

'There's no call for sarcasm. The tea party went extremely well — more or less,' she added under her breath.

But Jordan, being Jordan, heard her.

'What do you mean, more or less? What happened? Come on — tell.'

She'd often wondered if Jordan possessed some sort of extra hearing ability to everyone else; a kind of sixth sense. This seemed to prove that she did. Either that, or she could read minds. And if that were true, what chance did Lexie have of keeping anything secret? 'I didn't mean anything.'

'Oh, do you always speak with no meaning then? Can't say I've noticed,' Jordan bit back.

'It's just that I've agreed to go to the zoo next Sunday.' And that was all she was going to say. She had no intention of mentioning her and Bruno's kiss. Jordan would have a heyday with that piece of info. So much so, Lexie would never hear the last of it.

'You what?' Jordan hooted with laughter. 'You — going to the zoo? You don't even like zoos. You always say it's cruel.'

'I know, I know. But I didn't have the heart to refuse. Serena's such a lovely, sweet little girl. Anyway, I've promised to take Sally's daughter with me — Jennifer.'

'Does Sally know that?'

'Not yet. I'll ring her in a while. She'll agree. She's always moaning she doesn't have any time to herself.'

'O-kay. And is the gorgeous Mr Cavendish going on this trip too?'

'Yes.'

'Ha-ha. Methinks you have made a conquest.'

'Don't be stupid,' Lexie scoffed.

'Stupid? Why else would a man like him go to a zoo? I can't imagine it's his usual venue to visit. Oh yes,' she airily declared, 'he's definitely smitten.'

'He's doing it for his daughter.'

'Yeah, right,' Jordan scoffed. She clearly didn't believe that for a second. 'And what does Danny think of all of this?'

Lexie shrugged. 'I couldn't care less what Danny thinks.'

Jordan's glance sharpened. 'Have you two had a falling out?'

'You could say that, I suppose.' Lexie lowered her voice. She didn't want Alice or Mel overhearing her. 'I haven't seen

Danny in days.'

Jordan's mouth dropped open. 'You what? Where is he?'

'Haven't a clue. He's disappeared.'

'Disappeared?'

'Yeah, he didn't come home on Thursday night and hasn't been back since.'

'Well, has he phoned?'

'No. And his phone is permanently on an answering service.'

'Aren't you worried?'

'Not especially.' Which was, of course, a lie. 'It isn't the first time he's done this. To tell you the truth, I'm a bit fed up with Danny. It might be time to end things. And maybe that's why he's gone.'

'Wow!'

'Yeah, wow indeed. Now, I don't want to discuss him anymore, if you don't mind.'

Jordan frowned. 'Is he having an affair?'

'It's possible.' However, she had more or less discounted that, concluding that there was a lot more to Danny's disappearance than a mere affair, but she wasn't going to share that with Jordan either.

'Has he taken his things?'

'No, not yet.'

'He'll be back then. You know Danny.'

'Yeah, I suppose I do.'

'Anyway, to change the subject ...' Jordan narrowed her eyes at Lexie. 'You need to be careful of Bruno Cavendish, gorgeous or not. I've been asking around.'

Lexie rolled her eyes. 'There's a surprise.'

Jordan ignored that gibe and carried on. 'And it seems he's gained himself quite a reputation with regards to women. He loves 'em and leaves 'em, apparently. You really don't want to end up as one of his leavings.'

'I've no intention of getting involved with Bruno Cavendish.'

'Ri-ight.' For the second time in as many minutes, Jordan clearly didn't believe her. 'O-kay, so, changing the subject again, do you fancy a night out, just you and me? It would take your mind off things. Namely, Bruno Cavendish.'

'My mind isn't on Bruno Cavendish,' Lexie strenuously protested.

'Oh my, methinks the lady doth protest too much.'

'Oh, shut up.'

'Anyway, a new bistro has opened in Kingsford.' Kingsford was the nearest large town to Adlington, and it sported a plethora of restaurants, bistros, and even a nightclub. 'Shall we give it a go? The food's good and I've heard it's relatively cheap, so what do you think?'

'Oh, I don't know.'

'Go on. It might be fun, and you sound as if you need a bit of that.'

And Jordan was right. The truth was, Lexie did need some fun. To take her mind off next Sunday's trip to the zoo, if nothing else. 'Okay. You're on.'

* * *

Lexie duly rang her friend, Sally, who couldn't believe what it was she was asking.

'Bruno Cavendish!' she cried. 'How on

earth did you get to know him? He's the richest man in town.'

'I met him at the time of the break-in at the salon.' Lexie had decided not to comment on Bruno's financial status, mainly because she had no idea whether Sally's statement was a correct one — though if Jordan was to be believed, it most probably was.

'Oh yes, of course. The jeweller's next door to you. He lost all his stock, didn't he? I saw something about it on the local news.'

'Right.'

'Wow! Well, who am I to stop Jennifer socialising in such distinguished company? It's always good to know the rich and influential — who knows what they'll be able to do for you in the future? Hey, I've had a great idea. Maybe you'll introduce him to Pete and me sometime? We could all go and have a meal. What do you say, huh? He must have loads of useful contacts — Pete's a bit fed up with his job at the moment and is looking to have a change. Something with more money, chiefly.'

Lexie chose not to respond to any of this, other than to murmur noncommittally, 'Well.' She had no intention of introducing Bruno to any of her friends. That would place a significance on their relationship that she didn't want to foster. Her sole aim was to keep him at arm's length — though after their passionate kiss, that might prove a bit of a problem.

'Oh my God, it will be sheer bliss to have a bit of time to myself. I can have a bath in peace, a glass of wine, and then an afternoon nap. Pete's going to be out too.'

With that task successfully accomplished — though in the wake of Sally's overenthusiastic response and the difficulties that might result from it, she was starting to question whether she'd done the right thing — Lexie drove to Jordan's, and off they went.

At first sight, the bistro looked perfect: subdued lighting, beautifully laid tables with white linen cloths and a candle burning in the centre of each one, a log fire, and a refined murmuring of voices.

All very sophisticated. Too sophisticated? Had Jordan got this all wrong? It didn't strike Lexie as anything like a reasonably priced place. The exact opposite, in fact.

As if to emphasise this impression, a black-jacketed waiter greeted them just inside the door with a polite bow. 'Good evening, ladies. Do you have a reservation?'

'Oh.' Jordan looked taken aback. 'No, I didn't think we'd need one on a Monday evening.'

'Oh, dear, I'm so sorry,' the man said, 'but we are fully booked.'

'Really?' Jordan cried. 'But I can see an empty table over there.' She pointed across the room.

'Well, yes,' the waiter began,' but …'

'José,' a familiar voice said from behind them, 'if these ladies want, they can share our table. You don't mind, do you, Ben?'

Lexie swivelled, as did Jordan, and they found themselves face to face with none other than Bruno Cavendish and another equally good-looking man. He really did seem to have the knack of turning up at the most unexpected times.

'God, no. Two such lovely ladies. Who in their right mind would turn that down?' The man called Ben grinned broadly at them both.

Lexie had her mouth open ready to say 'Thank you, but we couldn't possibly impose' when Jordan, running true to form, leaped in to say, 'We'd love to share your table, wouldn't we, Lexie?' She nudged Lexie hard on her arm.

After a muted 'Ouch,' what else could Lexie do but agree? 'Um — well, do you mind? Only, we don't want to intrude.'

'Yes we do,' Jordan boldly contradicted her with a broad grin. 'We've heard the food's terrific here.' She fluttered her eyelids at the two men. 'As are the men with whom we'll be dining.' And she gave what she obviously thought was a seductive laugh, at the same time wiggling her hips and running her fingers through her mane of hair.

Lexie gave a low groan. This was going to be a hellish evening. Jordan wasn't the most discreet of women, as she'd already made more than evident. She glanced round the room. Every eye in the place seemed to be glued to them, some with amusement, but several with frowning disapproval.

However, both men laughed, although she noticed Bruno bestowing a narrowed glance her way. 'Lexie,' he murmured, 'are you okay with this?'

'Yes, fine.' Although, of course, she was far from fine.

'Okay.' He turned back to the waiter. 'Make it a table for four then, José.'

'Certainly, Mr Cavendish. If you will all enjoy a drink at the bar, I'll lay two extra places.'

Lexie waited apprehensively for whatever her friend decided to say or do next, determined to do whatever it took to hide her blushes if it should turn out to be something outrageous, even if it entailed the indignity of pretending she'd dropped her napkin and crawling beneath the table to retrieve it. But all Jordan did was to ensure she was sitting between the two men and proceed to flirt with both of them in turn.

'So, Bruno,' she said, widening her eyes at him, 'did you enjoy the tea party on Sunday? I know Lexie did.' She darted a provocative glance at her friend. 'Didn't you, Lex?'

Lexie took a deep breath and did not answer. Instead, she waited for whatever was about to come next.

'It lived up to every one of my expectations,' was all Bruno said.

Jordan's glance sharpened and her eyes darted to Lexie. 'Oh?'

'Serena, of course, loved it,' he went on. He was clearly not prepared to reveal anything of substance to the inquisitive Jordan, much to Lexie's relief.

Jordan, however, made no attempt to hide her disappointment at this lacklustre answer. 'And you?' She just couldn't help herself, Lexie reflected. She was like a dog with a bone. She had to extract every last morsel from it. 'Did you love it?'

But instead of answering that, Bruno went on, 'I've asked Lexie to join us for a trip to the zoo.' He'd kept a perfectly straight face throughout this brief inquisition, although Lexie did detect the increasingly familiar glint of amusement within his eye. He was fully aware of what Jordan was up to, and he wasn't about to pander to her curiosity.

'Hmmm.' Visibly frustrated by Bruno's impassivity, she gave up and turned her attention to Ben. 'So, do you and Bruno work together?'

'We do. I manage his business finances. An accountant, in other words. I keep him on the straight and narrow — or at least I try to.'

'So,' Bruno softly said to Lexie, who sat on his other side, 'did you manage to invite your friend's daughter on Sunday?'

'Yes, and she's coming. I just hope Serena gets on with her.'

'I'm sure she will.' He tilted his head the better to appraise her. 'I wondered if you'd stay for dinner with me afterwards?'

'I have to take Jennifer home,' she replied, grasping at the perfect and heaven-sent excuse to avoid what sounded dangerously like an intimate dinner for two — the very last thing she wanted, in light of their kiss last evening.

'I can get someone to do that. I keep a driver on standby.'

Of course you do, Lexie reflected with more than a touch of annoyance.

'He's utterly trustworthy,' he went on.

'I'm sure he is, but I'd rather do it myself, if you don't mind.'

'Tell you what, we'll drop her off on the way back to the manor. How's that?'

Lexie stared at him. Though there was no hint of anything to suggest that he was anticipating a repetition of their parting kiss the previous afternoon, he did seem very determined about this — which made her question exactly what he did have in mind for the evening. She recalled Jordan's warning about him. He liked to love 'em and leave 'em. Well, whatever he was planning, that wasn't going to happen to her. Definitely not. 'I don't know. I hadn't anticipated being out that late.'

'Why? Do you turn into a pumpkin if you're late home?' His features hardened and his eyes glinted, their expression unreadable. 'Or has the boyfriend returned?'

'No.'

'Then what?' His eyes narrowed now until they were no more than slits, once again making it impossible for Lexie to discern his thoughts. 'Is it me?'

She swallowed, nervous all of a sudden. 'No — yes. I-I've heard you have a bit of a reputation.' Oh God, had she just actually said that? She'd expect such bluntness from Jordan, but not from herself.

'Reputation? For what?' He looked genuinely bemused now. Perplexed, even.

'As-as a bit of a philanderer.'

He stared at her for a second or two, and then he gave a snort of something that sounded uncomfortably like contempt. 'A philanderer? What the hell does that mean?'

Lexie became aware of Ben's and Jordan's gazes sweeping towards them.

'If you mean I take a woman out occasionally, then yes, I'm guilty as charged. But that's it. I'm not out every night. I have a child to consider.' His tone was a savage one. 'I'd hardly call that philandering.'

'I didn't mean ...' Lexie felt the dreaded blush warming her face. She met Jordan's gaze beseechingly. *Help me*, she silently pleaded.

'That's probably my fault,' Jordan generously rushed to admit. 'I'd heard a rumour or two and told Lexie — well, warned her, if I'm absolutely honest.'

'Really.' Bruno's gaze flailed her.

'Yes. You're a bit of a ladies' man, apparently. Sorry, but you know what local gossip is like.'

Ben was laughing out loud by this time. 'Anyone less like a ladies' man than Bruno I can't imagine. He's the typical stay-at-home father. In fact, a monk probably has more fun than him. This is the first time in weeks he's been out of an evening, despite my persistent and frequent requests for him to join me.'

A rather uncomfortable silence followed this before Jordan leaped in and began to hastily talk once more, mainly to Ben. Bruno grabbed the opportunity to say to Lexie, 'As Ben has assured you that you'll be perfectly safe with me, will you dine with me on Sunday evening? If I promise to curb my baser instincts?' There was an expression in his eye now that in no way reassured Lexie. In fact, it did the exact opposite.

She regarded him. There was still a strange look to him, one of almost regret, and she found herself wondering if he was recalling their kiss. Maybe he too regretted it. Irrationally, she felt a sudden longing to have his arms around her and feel his lips on hers. 'Okay, if we can drop Jennifer home first.'

After that, the evening passed easily and pleasurably. The two men were clearly good friends; and Jordan, having made certain that Ben was single, made a determined play for him. He responded in kind, and Lexie wondered if she was witnessing the beginning of a relationship. She hoped so. Jordan was overdue a bit of happiness. Her last relationship had ended very acrimoniously twelve months ago and there'd been nobody since, which had made Lexie wonder more than once if that was the reason for her friend's acute interest in her and everyone else's lives.

When the time came for them all to go their separate ways, Bruno said, 'I'll see you on Sunday?'

'Yes, okay,' Lexie agreed.

'I'll pick you up at twelve o'clock. What's your address?'

* * *

Much to Lexie's astonishment, she wasn't subjected to an inquisition about Bruno on the way home. Jordan was way too busy talking about Ben and the possibility of seeing him again. Apparently he'd promised to ring her. Lexie prayed he would; otherwise, knowing her friend as she did, Jordan would be unbearable for a while.

It was three nights later that Lexie received another phone call. The same man's voice said, 'If you know what's good for you, you'd better tell me where Danny is. Otherwise I won't answer for the consequences.'

'Don't threaten me,' Lexie furiously interrupted. 'I don't know where he is — and what's more, I don't care. So when you find him, tell him he's not welcome here any longer.' And this time, she hung up.

7

It was as Lexie went to bed that she looked out of the sitting room window and saw the man's figure standing across the street. Just as last time, he didn't move; he simply stood staring at her. Without hesitating, she picked up the phone and called the police.

Two constables arrived within the hour, but of course whoever it had been was gone. Even so, she was a hundred percent sure it was the same man. One of the constables proceeded to ask the questions while the other wrote down Lexie's answers. She told them everything: that Danny had disappeared and that the stranger seemed to be stalking her, as well as making late-night phone calls, the most recent one containing a definite threat. And that she'd also suspected that someone other than Danny had been in the house on Sunday while she was out, although there didn't appear to be anything missing. She then told them that nothing of Danny's was missing either; that all of his clothes and belongings were still there.

'Do you have any idea why your partner would have disappeared?' the constable asked her. 'And why this person would be stalking you and threatening you? Entering your home — if that's what actually happened?'

He didn't bother hiding his scepticism at the supposed break-in. And she couldn't blame him. It had been five days ago and she was only just reporting it. She shook her head.

'Would your partner, Danny, have any reason for having you watched?'

'I can't think of one. But I don't think Danny's behind it, because this man is very keen to talk to him. He's looking for him, so whether Danny has done something to him, or taken something of his ... Actually, I'm starting to wonder whether Danny owes him money. Maybe that's what he was searching for — if he has been here. And it wouldn't be the first time Danny's been in serious debt and gone off for a while — to let the dust settle, so to speak, and tempers to cool.' She gave a weak smile. That bit about searching for money did sound rather improbable. No one would break into a place on the random chance of finding some money, would they? Not if they were owed a substantial amount. And it *must* be a substantial amount, judging by the manner in which the stranger was harassing her, even going so far as to threaten her. Or was she being naive? The truth was, she had no idea how the average thief thought.

'You didn't have a row then?'

'No, he just didn't come home on Thursday night.'

'If you were worried, why didn't you inform us of this earlier? It's been a week.'

'Well, I wasn't worried to begin with. He sometimes doesn't come home after a night out, not until the following morning; and as I've told already told you, this sort of thing has happened before. Once before.'

'Hmm.' He regarded her from beneath a lowered brow. For the second time, he wasn't making any attempt to hide his scepticism. 'And you say all his belongings are still here. He's taken nothing with him?'

'That's right. Um, I've been wondering — do you think he's had an accident or something?'

'We'll check with the hospitals, but I don't hold out much hope of that, Ms Brookes.' She didn't mention that she'd already rung several hospitals in the vicinity. An official enquiry might have a better chance of discovering if that was indeed what had happened. 'I'm pretty sure you would have been notified if that was the case. I'm afraid we have hundreds of people disappearing all the time. We don't have the resources or the funds to search for them, unless there's been evidence of foul play of course. And as for the man watching you ...' He shrugged. 'Unless we catch him in the act, there's not much we can do.'

* * *

Sunday came around much too quickly, mainly because the salon had been frantically busy all week. Lexie and Jordan had worked uncomplainingly, but Alice had grown sulkier by the day — well, by the hour, actually. She constantly moaned at Mel, the trainee, for not pulling her weight, not tidying up quickly enough, and keeping clients waiting to be shampooed, until in the end Lexie was forced to chastise her. Alice responded to that with a sullen silence that lasted for the rest of the day, not speaking to anyone, not even her clients, until she was forced to. However, that didn't prevent her gaze going repeatedly to the door each time it opened, her expression one of keen anticipation which instantly changed to frowning disappointment at whoever came in.

Eventually she'd asked Lexie, 'Where's Danny these days? He usually pops in once or twice during the week.'

Lexie regarded her, her suspicions about an affair between the two of them resurrecting themselves. It was an all-too-plausible scenario. Alice was an attractive woman, with her curvy figure and long blonde hair. It was just a shame that she had such a bad attitude to everything and everyone; an attitude that had been steadily growing worse. Lexie wondered again whether it was Danny's prolonged absence that was responsible. It would go a long way towards explaining her present moodiness. It would also indicate that Danny hadn't been in touch with her either — which only served to intensify Lexie's concern about where he was and what he was doing.

'He's busy,' was all she said, though the temptation to demand the truth from Alice about what — if anything — was happening between her and Danny was almost irresistible. However, resist it she did. She had no wish to expose her fears and uncertainties to Alice.

'Really?' Alice sneered. 'He hasn't left you, has he?'

Lexie stopped what she was doing. 'And why would you think that, Alice?' The insinuation couldn't be missed — that maybe Alice had good reason to ask that question.

Alice shrugged as a flush stained her cheeks. 'Dunno, really. Just ... things haven't looked too good between you lately, that's all.' And she swung back to her work.

But Lexie hadn't been able to stop herself from dwelling on the situation. Maybe Alice had threatened to tell Lexie what was going on, hoping to force Danny into leaving Lexie and going to her permanently. And if that was the case, it would be just like Danny to run away. As she'd told the constables, he'd done it before, just not for this long. Six months ago, he'd disappeared for several days after getting himself into debt with his credit cards. Instead of trying to work out some sort of repayment plan, he'd simply disappeared, just like he had now. He'd taken time off work and gone to Spain, without a word to Lexie. She'd been beside herself with worry until three days later, when he rang her and confessed the truth.

She'd helped him out then, but this time it was different. Someone was actively looking for him; someone who sounded and looked dangerous. As she'd mentioned to the police, could debt be behind this second disappearance? Did he owe money to the mysterious stranger? A stranger who was now hell-bent on getting that money back by one means or another, even if it meant breaking and entering — though there'd been no actual breaking of anything. And Lexie didn't even know for sure that there'd been any entering. Did that theory sound any more realistic than the one of Danny having an affair with Alice and then being forced to run from her? Not really. Of course, there was nothing to say he hadn't been seeing Alice as well. Maybe he'd borrowed the money to spend on her.

But whatever the reason for his disappearance, this time he'd gone too far.

* * *

When two days had passed and no call had come from the police, Lexie could only assume that they had no information to give her. That did seem to indicate that Danny hadn't been injured and admitted to hospital, which was a relief. Even though she was angry with him, she didn't wish him harm, whatever he'd been up to.

And now that Sunday had arrived, Lexie found herself bitterly regretting having agreed to go to the zoo with Bruno and Serena. Her anxiety about Danny had remained with her. She couldn't rid herself of the suspicion that the stranger was intending him some sort of harm. But she repeatedly told herself there was nothing more she could do to help him. She'd tried ringing him, she'd informed the police, and she'd enquired at hospitals, all of which had produced no results. If he'd come to harm, she'd have been told by now. She really had to get on with her life. She refused to go on putting this unpredictable man, this undeniably selfish man, above all else. He must know how she'd worry, but he hadn't spared her a single thought — that was more than obvious.

With that decision made, Lexie felt as if a weight had been lifted from her; and the fact was, she'd made a promise, and she'd never been one to renege on one, especially not one made to an adorable five-year-old. So in an attempt to ease her concerns about what might happen between herself and Bruno, she indulged in a long, hot bath before facing the problem of what to wear.

It had to be an outfit suitable for walking around a zoo, and then dining with Bruno at his home. She was quite sure he'd be accustomed to only being with women who wore expensive and exclusive designer wear. As she owned nothing remotely like that, she rifled through the array of clothes hanging in her wardrobe for a good fifteen minutes, finally deciding in a fit of desperation on a pair of plain slim-legged grey trousers and a silky aquamarine V-necked blouse. She teamed these with a pair of low-heeled black shoes and a three-quarter-length shower-proof jacket. As it was now October, the days had been growing progressively cooler and the weather had become more changeable. A glance through her window told her that it was heavily overcast at the moment, so she added a scarf to the outfit, just in case. She then stood back and viewed herself in the full-length mirror. Definitely not a designer look; more a high street look — M & S, in fact — but it would have to do.

She had only just completed her makeup and arranged her hair when the doorbell chimed. That would be Jennifer. Sally had promised to bring her by a quarter to twelve, and it was already five to.

Lexie hurried downstairs to open the front door, expecting to see her friend outside. Bruno stood there instead. 'Ready?' He smiled.

'Um — no. Jennifer's not here yet.' She

could see Serena sitting in the rear of a large silver Mercedes. The little girl waved to her. 'Will you both come in? I'll give Sally a ring.'

As she spoke, the phone rang. It was Sally. 'Sorry, sorry. We're running late. I'll be there in ten.'

'Okay.' Lexie swung around to see Bruno helping Serena from the car.

'Hi, Lexie,' the little girl called as she got closer. 'We're coming in, Daddy says.' She then lifted her face up towards Lexie, clearly inviting a kiss of welcome. Lexie willingly obliged, loving the feel of the satin-smooth skin beneath her lips, as well as the scent of freshly shampooed hair.

She straightened up and smiled apologetically at Bruno before leaning closer to him and whispering, 'Jennifer will be here in ten minutes.' She just hoped her friend wouldn't insist on coming in and being introduced to him. Sally could be every bit as outspoken as Jordan, although not quite as prone to outrageous innuendo.

'No worries,' he immediately assured her.

She led the way into the sitting room. It must look tiny in comparison to Adlington Manor's rooms, she reflected.

'Oh, how cute,' Serena cried.

'We-ell,' Lexie murmured, 'that's one description. Another would be small.'

'It's nice,' Bruno said. 'Cosy.'

Lexie's nervousness at having him here in her home began to get to her, and she rubbed both hands together. 'Please sit down.'

'Where's my surprise?' Serena asked. Lexie had been expecting the question. She'd noticed the girl's keen-eyed gaze around the room.

'Serena,' Bruno gently admonished.

'It'll soon be here.' Lexie checked the clock on the wall. It was almost ten past twelve. 'I hope,' she muttered.

'Lexie,' Bruno put in, 'there's no rush. We have all day at our disposal.' His glance then swept the room as well — searching for something? If he was, however, he didn't say anything. Lexie was relieved she'd put the photograph of herself and Danny in the bureau drawer.

Bruno would have zoomed in on that, she was sure.

'Your partner's not back then?' he asked, confirming her suspicion that he'd been looking for something. Evidence of Danny's presence?

'No,' she curtly said. She had no desire to talk about Danny, and certainly not with Bruno Cavendish.

He cocked his head and regarded her from narrowed eyes. 'Would he object to you coming out with me — us?' He swiftly amended his question.

Lexie could only suppose he'd interpreted her expression for what it was: an unwillingness to have their outing portrayed as a romantic date. 'Haven't a clue, but even if he did ...' She shrugged, and he could make what he wanted of that.

8

Bruno's gaze didn't leave her, his expression more than a little satisfied. So satisfied, in fact, it verged on smug. He'd clearly picked up on the unspoken fact that Lexie no longer cared what Danny thought, and that evidently pleased him.

'I'd offer you a drink ...' Lexie began. Then the doorbell rang and she hurried into the hallway. This time when she opened the door, Jennifer stood there. Lexie looked over her head to see Sally climbing back into her car. She swivelled and waved to Lexie, calling 'See you later,' and then she was gone again, eager obviously to make the most of the bath and glass of wine that she had waiting for her. Lexie breathed a gentle sigh of relief. With Bruno's car standing outside, she'd expected her to insist on coming in to meet him. She hadn't, so whatever she had waiting for her at home must be pretty damn good.

'Come in, Jennifer,' Lexie whispered, putting a finger to her mouth to warn the little girl that she mustn't say anything, not yet. 'I've someone in here who's longing to meet you.' She took hold of Jennifer's hand and led her into the sitting room. 'Serena, meet Jennifer.'

Serena looked more than surprised, she looked positively astonished. 'Is this my surprise?'

Lexie couldn't tell whether she was pleased or disappointed. Her heart sank. Had she got it all wrong? But then a huge grin lit up Serena's features and she ran towards Jennifer. 'Are you coming to the zoo with us?' She reached out a hand to Jennifer, who took it.

'Yes, I am.'

'Wow! This is mega. Thank you, Lexie.' She turned and hugged Lexie around the hips.

'I'm glad you're pleased,' Lexie laughed, impulsively meeting Bruno's gaze as she did so.

His response startled her. His eyes

instantly narrowed as his face paled, the blood draining dramatically from it. He looked ... well, winded, she supposed. But then in the next second, he too was grinning, and she wondered if she'd imagined that briefly stunned look.

'This has sealed your place right at the top of the popularity stakes,' he said. After a pause, he softly added, 'And not just Serena's either.'

Lexie's face warmed as his gaze lingered on her, his eyes smouldering beneath their lowered lids, the desire within them unmissable.

With the introductions over, they went out to Bruno's car. Lexie sighed enviously at the sheer luxury of it as she settled herself into the front passenger seat.

Bruno slanted a glance at her and asked, 'Are you comfortable enough?'

'I'll say. Luxuriously so,' she breathed.

He gave a soft laugh. 'Good. I aim to please.'

She only just stopped herself from saying, 'Oh, you do that all right.' She couldn't imagine how he'd react to that sort of response from her. Or rather she could, only too well. He'd interpret her words as encouragement to kiss her again. And, all of a sudden, that possibility didn't seem in any way undesirable.

As the car moved away from the kerbside, the large engine purred like a well-fed cat. Lexie was tempted to do the same.

Bruno glanced at her. 'I know a rather nice pub we could have a spot of lunch at. There's no problem about taking the children inside. Does that sound okay?'

'It does. It sounds wonderful, actually.'

And it did. She could live like this all the time: a luxurious car to travel in, and a man who considered her wishes before his own. In fact, Bruno was turning out to be the exact opposite of Danny, who'd been treating her with casual indifference for the past few months, disregarding her wishes, disappearing for hours on end — and now for ten days, without as much as a phone call. As for their sex life, that was practically nonexistent, and had been for a while. But with Bruno she felt treasured; cared for. Precious, in fact. Why shouldn't she enjoy that while she could? She couldn't stop another sigh, deeper this time.

Bruno turned his head. 'Everything okay?'

'Oh, yes. Everything's very okay.' She smiled warmly at him, watching as for a second time his face paled and he was forced to take a deep breath.

Within another ten minutes, they were pulling into the car park of a black-timbered, white-walled thatched pub. Its small diamond-paned and leaded windows gleamed and shone in an unexpected shaft of sunlight. A spirited breeze was shooing the clouds away, making Lexie hope that it heralded a warmer day. It would make exploring the zoo a much more enticing prospect than that of walking beneath leaden skies with the unwelcome risk of rain.

Serena and Jennifer hadn't stopped talking the entire way. Lexie looked back at them now. They were delighted with each other. It had been a brainwave to ask Jennifer along — a sentiment Bruno promptly endorsed.

'This was a truly wonderful idea of yours,' he said. 'I can't thank you enough. I haven't seen Serena this animated in a long time.'

Lexie gazed at him and softly asked, 'Does she see much of her mother?'

Bruno's expression darkened and his tone hardened. 'No. She's living on the Costa del Sol with her new husband, and I'm told they haven't got the time to come back more than once a year. He's got business interests down there. Something to do with the timeshare market, I'm not sure what exactly. They haven't been back at all this year.'

'Serena must miss her.' Lexie's heart ached for the small girl, all but abandoned by her mother. Maybe that was why she was so affectionate towards Lexie — she was desperate for a woman's care and attention; for her love. Bruno should really see about finding a suitable nanny for her. A housekeeper, taking all her other duties into account, wasn't good enough — with the best will in the world, she wouldn't have the time. Lexie wondered whether she should suggest it.

But before she could do so, Bruno said, 'I'm not sure she does. Natalie wasn't a stay-at-home mother. She much preferred to pay a nanny and go to work.' He shrugged. 'Sadly, the nanny left to get married shortly after Natalie left. I've tried to find someone else but haven't had any luck at all.'

'I see. Well, we must make sure she enjoys today, then. She and Jennifer have really hit it off. We'll have to make sure they meet again.' Lexie abruptly stopped as she realised what it was she'd just said. Her impulsive words had undoubtedly given the impression that she, Bruno and Serena would be meeting up on a regular basis.

And that was exactly how Bruno interpreted them, for he turned to her and murmured, 'That sounds like a promise to come out with us again.'

'I'm sorry, that was presumptuous of me. I didn't mean ...'

He gave her a droll look. 'Did you not? In that case, I'm deeply disappointed.'

She didn't know what to say to that.

'I want to see you again, Lexie.'

'Well . . .' She frowned. Maybe it was time to come clean about Danny and what was happening. But that would make her sound like the sort of woman who consorted with men who'd just up and disappear without a word. In particular, a man who was also being stalked, and whose stalker was threatening her. No, she couldn't tell him. He'd despise her. And in any case, how could she become romantically involved with him — which it was becoming increasingly evident that he wanted — while she didn't know where Danny was or what had happened to him? What would he think of her then? The same as he thought of his uncaring wife, probably. And she wouldn't be able to bear that.

'Well? Well what?' His tone was a throaty one.

'As I told you, I am involved with someone else.'

'Yes, someone who doesn't seem to be around at the moment. Tell me, how long are you prepared to wait for him to return?'

'I don't know.' Her eyes widened at him. 'S-sorry.'

'For what?'

'What?'

'What are you sorry for? You keep saying it.'

'Oh, I see. Well, I'm sorry that I can't give you an answer, I suppose.'

He regarded her intently then. 'Yet here you are, with me.'

'Yes.' She looked away from his penetrating stare. Was he judging her; implying that she wasn't being honest with him? Which, of course, she wasn't. 'I-I'm sorry.'

'Again?'

She returned her gaze to him and said the only thing she felt she could. 'If you want to call today off . . .'

'I don't.'

'You don't?'

'No. We can't disappoint the children,

can we?' Heavy lids veiled his expression, making Lexie wonder if it was only the children he was considering, or whether he himself would be disappointed too. She rather thought, taking into consideration his earlier remark, that he would be.

'No, I suppose not,' she said. He was right, of course, but she still couldn't help wondering if it was only the children he was thinking of.

'Lexie, I like being with you, and if that's all I can have for the moment, then that's okay. But when you decide what you want, or who you want, just say the word. Okay?'

She smiled shakily. 'Okay.' She couldn't mistake his meaning. If she wanted him, she could have him. She drew a long, slow breath at the mere idea.

He swivelled his head towards the two girls sitting patiently in the back seat. 'So, who's hungry?'

'I am,' they sang in perfect unison.

He grinned at Lexie. 'They must have been rehearsing.' Then he glanced back at the eager-faced children. 'Right — out you get then, and let's feed you.'

* * *

Lunch was swiftly consumed, so keen were the two girls to get to the zoo. Jordan had been absolutely right — Lexie didn't like zoos; they made her feel guilty and uncomfortable. It seemed terribly cruel to her to keep wild animals, who would have been free to roam vast expanses if they weren't in captivity, penned in.

However, to her immense pleasure, at this zoo that wasn't the case. The conditions the animals would have enjoyed in the wild were faithfully replicated, as far as possible. They were living in large areas filled with the sorts of trees, plants and grasses that would surround them in their natural habitats; and Lexie had to admit that, despite the enclosures, they all looked perfectly content and very happy — probably because they were totally safe from any sort of predator. So in a way, this zoo could be regarded as contributing to their welfare and the continuation of their species, which wasn't a bad thing.

They spent three hours wandering around, the two children excitedly pointing out things to each other as well as Bruno and Lexie. A couple of times people smiled at the girls and said to Lexie and Bruno, 'What lovely children you have. You must be very proud.'

On the first occasion, Lexie started to say 'Oh no, they're not', only to have Bruno grasp her hand and squeeze her fingers as if to say, *No, don't.* She looked at him quizzically. He smiled and whispered, 'Don't spoil it. It feels great to be mistaken for a normal, happy family.'

So full of longing was his expression that her heart ached, and she found herself unexpectedly wishing, like him, that they were truly a family. With the result that the second time it happened, she merely smiled at the other people and mouthed 'Thank you.'

Children were something she and Danny had never discussed. She'd always known she wanted them at some time, but that time never seemed to come. Was that because she'd always believed she and Danny wouldn't last? Had she, in fact, always sensed that it would end sometime?

Now, looking at Serena and Jennifer darting excitedly about, chattering non-stop, and pointing out things to each other, Lexie was pierced by a deep and unexpected longing to have her own child. That couldn't happen, though — not with the way things were at the moment. And certainly not with Danny. She'd never be sure he wouldn't disappear again, leaving her with a child or children to bring up on her own.

* * *

By the time they returned to the car, darkness was beginning to descend, and the zoo staff were making preparations to close up. The two girls were visibly tired, and within a couple of minutes of getting back in the car they were both sound asleep.

'First time they've stopped talking,' Bruno remarked. 'Do you think your friend would let Jennifer visit Serena at home?'

Lexie hesitated. Bruno was, after all, a single man, and nowadays one had to be so careful. But she was almost sure that Sally wouldn't refuse. Still, playing safe, all she said was, 'I'll ask her, if you like.'

'Oh, I'd like — as long as you come along too, when you can of course.'

She widened her eyes at him. He didn't miss a trick, did he?

'Will you stop doing that?' he roughly said.

'Stop doing what?' She was genuinely puzzled by his words. What was she doing?

'Widening your eyes at me.' His voice was low and throaty. 'You have no idea what it does to me.'

She couldn't help herself then. 'What does it do to you?' Her words came out as husky as his had been. She knew she was being provocative, but she wanted to know.

He stared at her, his head to one side. 'It sends every nerve ending in my body haywire. So much so that I ache to kiss you and hold you.' His lids lowered over eyes that were blazing with passion. 'You have no idea how beautiful you are, do you? How bloody sexy?'

That brought her down to earth with a bump. Was that all it was? All he wanted? Sex?

'I see.' She was well aware that her tone was one of displeasure, censure, disappointment — but she didn't care. It wasn't mere sexual gratification that she wanted from him; she could get that anywhere and with anyone she chose. Sexual desire alone was fleeting, inevitably dulling once the initial excitement dimmed. She knew that only too well from her life with Danny. If that was all Bruno wanted from her ...

He was studying her intently. 'I'm very attracted to you, Lexie. I'd like a relationship with you. I ...' He stopped talking at that point and she wondered what he'd been about to say. 'But you're with someone else, I know.'

'Yes, I am,' she bluntly said. She was tempted to tell him that the last thing she needed was mere sex with another man; that what she really wanted was a love that would last a lifetime. But of course she didn't, because she was beginning to suspect that that wasn't what Bruno was offering, and she wasn't prepared to humiliate herself by revealing that desire. 'I think you'd better take me home once we've dropped Jennifer off.'

She saw his double take and his look of disbelief. 'If I've upset you, I apologise. I thought you realised how I felt.'

'You haven't upset me.' She was trying, with everything in her, to remain detached and unemotional. 'I-I just think it might be best.'

'You have nothing to fear from me. Please, come and have dinner with me. Serena will be very disappointed if you return straight home.'

That was underhanded, she decided furiously — using Serena to plead his case.

'I'll be on my best behaviour, I promise.'

He was making fun of her, she realised. She could practically see his tongue in his cheek. He'd be pledging scout's honour next.

'I won't lay a finger on you, if that's what you want.'

But was it what she wanted? She was no longer sure. And actually, so what if it was just sex as far as he was concerned? She hadn't had a man make love to her — passionately, as she was quite sure Bruno would — for too long. Certainly Danny hadn't, which had been what had aroused her suspicion of an affair in the first place. He'd always been a very physical man, wanting — no, needing — to satisfy his sexual desires on a regular basis. But deep down, she knew that casual sex wasn't for her; wasn't what she wanted. It had to be more than that, otherwise what was the point? But then again, when was the last time she'd had fun with a man? And sex could be fun, with the right person.

'Lexie, please. I'll let you decide how we do things; you can call the shots. You have my word on that.' Suddenly Bruno was deadly serious, and Lexie questioned her certainty that he'd been poking fun at her just moments ago. 'I don't want Serena disappointed either. She's really taken to you. She's been let down too many times in her short life.'

And that was the clincher. Lexie did not want to disappoint the little girl either. 'Okay,' she agreed, albeit reluctantly. 'But it's just dinner, nothing else.'

'Just dinner. I promise.'

However, her sideways glance at him didn't reassure her, not one little bit. He was looking way too pleased with himself for comfort.

With that settled — at least Lexie hoped it was — they dropped Jennifer off at home. This time Sally insisted on coming out to the car and being introduced to Bruno. Her greeting and thanks for taking Jennifer out were embarrassingly gushing. Lexie could only be grateful that Bruno didn't appear to notice. He behaved with his usual smooth charm, smiling broadly even when Sally tried to insist they come inside for a drink.

'Pete would love to meet you. He actually stayed at home and missed the footie.' She gave a tiny suggestive wink to Lexie.

Lexie grinned at her. So she'd been right — Sally had rushed off earlier because she did have something good waiting for her at home: Pete, by the sound of it. Lexie was quite sure they'd taken full advantage of their small daughter's absence for the afternoon.

'Sorry, Sal,' she said. 'We have to get Serena home, but thanks anyway.'

They'd been driving for several minutes before Bruno asked, 'How long have you known Sally?'

'Oh, years. Longer than I've known Jordan. We started school together. Our mums had been friends for years as well.'

'Do you think she'd allow Jennifer to come and have a sleepover? Now that she's met me, so to speak. Though it was a pretty brief meeting.'

Lexie eyed him. 'Um — did you want to go in for a drink? Only, I thought of Serena and school tomorrow. That you wouldn't want her to be late to bed.' Her words petered out. Had he been implying that she should have asked him before turning Sal's invitation down?

'No, no. I was just wondering, you know. And well, not to blow my own trumpet …'

Lexie almost laughed out loud at that. Here was the most self-assured, confident man she'd ever met telling her he wasn't blowing his own trumpet. He didn't have to. Everyone in the town knew how successful he was, Sally included. Lexie was quite sure by this point that she herself would bring Jennifer for a sleepover and probably beg to stay as well. She'd love nothing more than to have her daughter recognised by all and sundry as a close friend of Serena Cavendish.

'… but she did seem to approve of me, didn't she?' Bruno finished.

Again, Lexie had to struggle to stop herself from laughing. 'Oh yes, she approved of you all right. I'm sure she'd let Jennifer come.' Approve of him? Sally had been practically grovelling to him.

By the time they got to Adlington Manor, Lexie was trembling with nerves. She wouldn't be surprised if Bruno had had his fingers crossed behind his back as he'd made his promise. *Oh, for goodness sake*, she crossly thought, *what's wrong with me?* She was perfectly capable of handling Bruno Cavendish. But was she? According to Jordan, he'd had numerous women, and no matter how vehemently he denied that, she could tell he was accustomed to getting his own way — a skill that only came with a great deal of practice. Look at how he'd played her. Yes, she then conceded, but look at how unsure he was about Sally allowing Jennifer to come for a sleepover. So maybe he wasn't always as confident as he looked. Somehow that made him more appealing to her, more human than the Superman he sometimes appeared to be.

'Okay, here we are,' he said. 'Out you get, Serena. You can go and tell Ruthie all about our day out. She'll be dying to hear. Oh, and tell her we'll have dinner at eight.'

Serena danced off, visibly keen to relate every detail of her trip to the zoo. Bruno led Lexie into the room she'd been in before when she'd come to tea. The fire was lit and the lights were already dimmed. Ruthie must have been in and done it — on instructions from her employer? Lexie wondered. A quiver of unease went through her.

'Ruthie will give Serena her supper, so make yourself comfortable.' He indicated the settee. She made a point of sitting in an armchair, determined to make things clear right from the start. She noted the quivering of his lips, though, and wondered if that denoted amusement or irritation. The latter, probably. She couldn't imagine many people had frustrated his intentions.

'I'll get us a drink. Glass of wine, or something stronger? To bolster your courage.' He openly grinned.

Of course he'd seen straight through

her. So much for her earlier assumption that, just maybe, he wasn't always as sure of himself as he seemed. He certainly seemed to have no trouble detecting her emotions, and her thoughts, even. She tried to imagine living with someone that perceptive. It once again reinforced her decision to keep him at arm's length, no matter how much charm he employed. 'I'll have a glass of red wine, please.'

'Fine. I have a couple of bottles right here.'

'I don't think I'll be drinking that much,' she said. 'Have to keep my wits about me.'

'Why's that?' Knowing amusement glittered at her.

'One never knows what will happen, does one?' she bit back.

'I suppose one doesn't.' Amusement still gleamed in his eyes, and he was making no attempt to hide it. Irritation pierced Lexie once more. The man was impossible; maddeningly impossible.

He handed her the glass that he'd only half filled. 'Don't want you losing your wits, do we?' He grinned rakishly at her, clearly not meaning it. Then he poured himself a gin and tonic before sitting down on the settee and raising his glass to her. 'Here's to us, and a *very* good evening.'

Lexie stiffened. What the hell did that mean? She'd known she shouldn't come, and yet she'd allowed him to override her reservations.

'Relax,' he then said. 'It's just a casual toast. Nothing to worry about.'

She didn't believe him for a single second. With that in mind, she limited herself to a very small sip of the wine, only to decide to hell with it. She was here now, so she might as well enjoy herself. She took a larger mouthful.

'Atta girl,' Bruno encouraged her, not bothering to try and disguise the gleam in his eye.

Defiantly, she took another sip and felt her head begin to spin. She quickly replaced the glass on the table. That was more than enough for the time being. Who knew what would happen if she became intoxicated?

She should go — right now. Somehow, though, she couldn't muster the will to do so. In fact, she'd love nothing more than to curl up in her supremely comfortable chair and go to sleep. Her eyelids slowly drooped. It was only Bruno's voice that stopped her from dozing off.

'Did you enjoy your day at the zoo?'

'I did. I wasn't expecting to. I'm not usually a lover of the zoo.'

'Aren't you?' He took a mouthful from his own glass, all the while watching her across the rim.

'No. I can't bear to see wild animals penned up, but they weren't really. They were free to roam at will, in large enclosures, and I could see they were perfectly happy with that. And I suppose it could be regarded as a sort of conservation area. You know, protecting the animals from poachers as well as predators.'

'That's one way of looking at it. Anyway, I'm glad you enjoyed it.'

And that was the way things continued. Lexie's uncertainty about what the evening might bring faded, especially when Serena entered the room, already in her pyjamas, to bid them both goodnight. Lexie kissed her warmly.

'Lexie, will you come and read me a story?'

'Of course I will.' She'd be glad of a breathing space. The more wine she drank, the more intense her emotions became. She needed food, lots and lots of food, and it was still forty-five minutes to dinner. So an interlude with Serena was just the ticket.

She went upstairs with the little girl and onto a huge landing; there was an abundance of doors leading off it. 'How many bedrooms are there?' she asked, not wanting to be seen actually counting them.

'Oh, lots,' Serena airily told her. 'Nine, ten, something like that.'

'That's a great many bedrooms for just two people.'

'Well, Mummy comes and stays sometimes. But not often.' Her small face broke into a frown. 'And Granny and

Grandpa. And Daddy brings friends back too.'

Aah. Lexie let out a long, slow breath. Out of the mouth of a babe — the truth, finally. Bruno brought women back here for the night. Not that they would use one of the guest rooms, she angrily thought. Well, she had no intention of becoming one of the women who came and stayed overnight. Not in a million years.

Serena, blissfully unaware of what she'd just revealed, took hold of Lexie's hand and led her into a large, beautifully decorated bedroom. It had what looked like scenes from various fairytales painted onto the walls. It must have cost a fortune, because it had clearly been hand-painted by a highly talented artist. A child-sized canopied bed sat against one wall, surrounded by an exquisite painting of a forest. And was that Hansel and Gretel wandering through it, hand in hand? Red Riding Hood was identifiably there, basket over her arm. And there was Snow White with her seven dwarfs.

Lexie dragged her gaze away to a small

dressing table flanked by twin sets of shelves, each fully stocked with books and boxed games. There was a wooden rocking horse with a long mane the colour of clotted cream, and a tail to match, also hand-crafted. And a similarly exquisite doll's house. Dolls and soft toys were propped against the pillows on the bed, their glassy eyes seeming to stare directly at Lexie. In fact, there was everything a child could desire, right here in this room. It was the bedroom of a much-loved child.

'What a gorgeous room,' she said.

Serena leaped into bed and then patted the cover for Lexie to sit down. There was a book already selected for her to read. 'What have we here?' She picked it up.

'Cinderella,' Serena said. 'My favourite.'

'Right.' She glanced down at the small girl, sitting patiently and waiting for her to start reading. 'Are you comfortable?'

'Ye-es,' Serena sang out.

'Then I'll begin,' she solemnly said. She opened the book and began to read.

Serena half sat and half lay, listening intently, closely studying each picture as Lexie turned the pages. Lexie enjoyed reading aloud, and she assumed the voices of each character as she did so. At least, the voices as she thought they'd sound. Serena was entranced.

They were almost halfway through when Lexie became aware of someone else's presence. She raised her gaze from the pages and saw Bruno leaning in the doorway, one shoulder propped against the wooden jamb, his legs crossed at the ankles as he sipped from his glass. His eyes were half closed — hooded, in fact, as he watched Lexie and his daughter. But then his mouth widened in a tender smile.

'Daddy, Daddy,' Serena joyfully cried, 'come and sit here on the bed. We can be a real family, can't we? Just like we were at the zoo. Ple-ease, Daddy. You can marry Lexie and she can be my new mummy. You could have a baby, a sister for me.'

9

Appalled at the words that were cascading from Serena's lips, Lexie stopped reading and watched, frozen, as Bruno strode across to the bed. What was he going to do or say? She waited, her breath snagged in her throat. What *could* he say, other than to tell his daughter no? And then how would Serena react? Lexie had witnessed the evidence of a healthy temper a couple of times when the little girl couldn't get her own way. And she now looked so full of joy, of hope — both of which could change in a second to tears of frustration.

But, seemingly unperturbed by his daughter's demand, Bruno sat on the opposite side of the bed to Lexie and took hold of Serena's hand, then gently said, 'Darling, that's just not possible.'

'Why not?' Serena wailed.

'We-ell, Lexie already has someone in

her life.'

'No she hasn't, otherwise she wouldn't be here with us.'

For the second time, Lexie could only think, *out of the mouth of a babe.* Serena had gone straight to the nub of things. She could see nothing wrong with what she'd proposed.

Bruno could only glance across at Lexie and mouth, *Sorry.*

She shook her head at him as if to say, *Don't worry about it. I understand.*

'Serena,' Bruno went on, 'it's just not possible to always have what you want.'

'You do,' she retaliated. Lexie was forced to hide a smile.

'That's different,' Bruno told her. 'I'm an adult. I can make things happen — well, most of the time. But not always.' He gave Lexie a meaningful look. 'Sometimes other people's wishes and needs stop me from doing that.'

Serena now turned to Lexie. 'Do you want to marry my daddy?'

Lexie stared at her. What the hell could she say to that? 'Um — well, it's as your daddy says. I can't. I'm with someone else.'

'So where is he?' Serena folded her arms across her chest, her expression a defiantly demanding and very determined one. For a five-year- old, she was far too knowing; too confident by half — something else to add to the authoritarian manner she'd clearly inherited from Bruno. In a few years' time, there'd be no stopping her, and Bruno would really have his work cut out controlling her. Lexie couldn't prevent her smile at the sequence of images that that notion generated. But for now, she had to convince Serena that what she wished for simply couldn't happen.

'He's away at the moment,' she said.

'Does he know you're going out with my daddy?'

'N-no, he doesn't, because I haven't been able to speak to him. And I haven't actually been going out with your daddy. I've been going out with you.'

But Serena wasn't about to be fobbed off with that feeble argument. She lowered her brow and asked, 'Has he left you?'

Lexie glanced sideways at Bruno then. His expression was one of interested, very interested, speculation. 'Yes,' he softly murmured, 'I'd like to know the answer to that question too.'

Lexie glared at him. Between the two of them, they'd placed her in a very awkward position. She took a steadying breath and gave the only answer she could. 'Not as far as I know.' Which was perfectly true. She didn't know, not for sure.

Bruno gave her a gently pitying look. 'Anyway, that aside, don't you want Lexie to finish the story, Serena?'

Serena, knowing when she was beaten, replied, 'Yes, okay.' It was a grudging response, but one that Lexie gave mute thanks for.

Then Bruno returned his gaze to her and said, 'As soon as you've finished reading, dinner's ready. You don't mind if I stay and listen, do you?' And she knew she wasn't out of the woods yet. The last person she wanted listening to her silly voices was Bruno.

'If-if you want?'

'I do. You see, I particularly like the part where the handsome prince dances with Cinderella. It's something I've always wanted to do — dance with such a beautiful woman. My dream woman.' He gave an exaggerated sigh at that.

Serena clapped her hands. 'You can dance with Lexie if you like. I'll hum a tune.'

Bruno got to his feet and held out his arms to Lexie. 'Shall we?'

She glared. What had got into him? She should stand her ground and refuse. But when Serena began to hum some unrecognisable tune, and Bruno murmured 'You don't want to disappoint Serena, do you', what else could she do but place the book on the bed and get to her feet?

Mutely vowing that she'd get this over with as fast as possible, she walked into his arms, rigorously avoiding his amused gaze. But that didn't seem to matter, because he immediately began to waltz with her, swinging her round and round — in case she changed her mind, she guessed, which she was hugely tempted to do. But it didn't take her long to realise she was still in serious trouble as he pulled her close and pressed his mouth into her hair, his warm breath fanning her face and despatching shivers of excitement all the way through her. All the time, Serena kept humming. The two of them waltzed around the bedroom, Bruno still spinning them both as he did so, until all of a sudden Lexie felt disorientated and dizzy. Abruptly, she stopped dancing.

Serena stopped humming and Bruno held Lexie away from him. 'Are you okay? You're very pale.'

'I-I'm a bit dizzy, that's all. Could we stop now?'

He led her back to the bed and sat her down. 'Put your head down between your knees,' he instructed her. 'I must say, I've never had quite such a dramatic effect on a woman before. I don't know whether to be flattered or horrified.'

With her nausea receding, Lexie raised her head and regarded him. 'Take it from me,' she bit out, 'it wasn't down to you, other than for the fact that you kept spinning me round and round. I lost my sense of balance, my centre of gravity.'

He frowned then — whether from anxiety or guilt, Lexie couldn't have said. 'I'm sorry, Lexie, I didn't realise. Do you feel okay now?'

'Yes, thank you.'

'You needn't read any more of the story,' Serena kindly told her. 'Take her downstairs, Daddy, and give her a drink.'

'That sounds like a very good idea, darling,' Bruno said. 'Now, thank Lexie for reading to you.'

'Thank you, Lexie.' Serena held her face up for a goodnight kiss.

Lexie willingly obliged. 'I'll see you again soon, sweetheart,' she said. 'Go to sleep now.'

'I will, and I'll dream of your and Daddy's wedding day,' Serena said, with a look of innocent expectation. 'With me as bridesmaid.' And she snuggled down beneath her duvet and closed her eyes. 'I love you,' she whispered.

'I love you too,' Lexie whispered back.

She silently followed Bruno down the stairs and back into the snug, where Bruno said, 'Thanks for all of that, and I'm sorry. Serena shouldn't have said what she did. I don't know where she gets these ideas from.'

'Don't you?' Even to her own ears, she sounded sceptical. She wouldn't put it past Bruno to have fostered at least some of the notions. After all, who better than a small girl, whom he must see Lexie was growing increasingly fond of, to champion his desire for a relationship with her?

But he almost at once put paid to that theory, making her wonder rather uneasily if once again he'd interpreted her thoughts. 'No. Well, I have a suspicion. She must miss her mother — at times, at any rate; or at least misses having some sort of mother figure around.'

'What about Ruthie? She seems very fond of her.'

'Ruthie hasn't got the time to spend with her.'

'In that case, shouldn't you try again

to find her another nanny? Someone who could devote herself solely to her?'

'As I told you, I have tried. I interviewed half a dozen, and I wouldn't have let a single one of them look after a cat, let alone my only daughter.' He eyed Lexie for a long moment. 'She's becoming very fond of you, as you've probably guessed.'

'Yes. But I'd be absolutely useless as a nanny.'

'I wasn't thinking of asking you to be her nanny.' He quirked an eyebrow at her.

Before she could ask him what he meant by that, however, the door into the snug opened and Ruthie poked her head in. 'Dinner is ready if you are.'

'Oh, fine. Thank you, Ruthie, we're just coming.' He held out a hand to Lexie. 'We're eating in the dining room. Let me escort you.' And he crooked an elbow for her to thread her arm through.

As they walked into the hallway, Lexie found herself still wondering what he had been thinking of asking her.

Bruno led her into the dining room and towards a table that would have easily seated fifteen or sixteen people. However, it was only laid for two at one end, with silver cutlery, crystal wine glasses, huge dinner serviettes, two large candlesticks with their candles already lit, and a massive bowl of white-and-bronze chrysanthemums. Music was playing softly in the background, something classical that Lexie didn't recognise.

She glanced around the room once she'd taken her seat and saw light oak wainscoting and large oil paintings — landscapes this time, rather than portraits — on the plainly painted walls above the panelling. A fire burned in what looked like a genuine Adam fireplace — not that Lexie was any sort of expert in that particular field of knowledge.

'This is lovely,' she said.

Bruno looked pleased. 'Thank you. We've tried to keep the renovations in the period of the original house.'

We? Did he mean himself and his wife?

'By 'we', I mean my interior designer and myself. He specialises in restoring period houses.'

This was getting downright creepy — it was beginning to look as if he definitely had the ability to read her mind. She wondered nervously what else he might have detected. Her steadily growing feelings for him?

The door opened then, successfully distracting her from her disturbing reflections, and Ruthie walked in, bearing two plates which she set before them before, saying, 'Smoked salmon mousse.'

'It looks wonderful,' Lexie enthused. A perfectly formed dome of pale pink mousse was set on a bed of mixed salad leaves and miniature plum tomatoes; and four of the largest prawns she'd ever seen, thankfully out of their shells, decorated the edge of the plate.

Ruthie beamed. 'Enjoy.'

Once the housekeeper had left again, Bruno poured Lexie a glass of white wine. She took a cautious sip. She'd already drunk a large glass of red, so she really should show some restraint now. More than a couple of glasses and her head would spin and her tongue begin to run away with itself.

'Pinot Grigio,' Bruno told her.

'Lovely,' she said, sinking her fork into the delicious-looking mousse. 'Mmm, positively gorgeous,' she moaned softly, before demolishing the entire plateful in a matter of minutes. Bruno watched her, looking slightly bemused. 'Sorry.' God, he must think her an absolute pig. He'd barely touched his yet. 'I was starving.'

'Please, don't apologise. I like to see a woman relish her food. It's a refreshing change. So many today just nibble at the edges, frightened to death they'll gain a few pounds.'

She stared at him in dismay. Was he implying she was fat? All right, she wasn't thin, but she didn't consider herself fat either. Or maybe he was talking about his ex-wife?

'But,' he went on, 'you clearly don't need to worry about such a thing. You're just right.'

He'd done it again. She didn't need to put anything into words; all she had to do was think them and he knew exactly what was going on in her head. Creepy wasn't the word; downright terrifying was a much more apt description.

He finished his food then and leant back in his chair, his long fingers toying with the stem of his glass. He had nice fingers, she decided, at the same time quite unable to help wondering how they'd feel on her body. Oh God — supposing he'd sensed that question? She shivered, and it wasn't simply at the notion of him caressing her.

But if he had interpreted her thoughts, he didn't give any indication of it. Instead he asked, 'How's the salon doing? You haven't talked about it.'

'It's good. We've had a busy week, so the days have sped by.' But she didn't want to talk any more about herself; she was becoming terrified she'd inadvertently reveal too much — especially about her feelings for him. 'I've been wondering, have you heard anything about your stolen jewellery? Has any of it been recovered?'

'Not a thing. It's all long gone, for

sure. The matching sets and clusters of jewels have probably been split up into individual pieces and sold on by now. It was all insured; but even so, it's been a bit of a hassle having to restock. The shelves are still a little bare, but things are slowly getting back to normal. Anyway, enough about that. Tell me a bit about yourself; your family.'

'There's not much to tell. I have a father, John. My mother died three years ago. Brain tumour.' Her eyes clouded as they always did when she spoke about her mother. She still missed her dreadfully; missed being able to talk over her problems with her. For instance, she'd have been able to tell her about Danny, and now about her growing feelings for this man sitting opposite her. Her mother would have had the right words, reassuring words, putting all of Lexie's worries and concerns into perspective. She'd been great for that.

'My father owns a couple of estate agencies, here in Adlington and in Kingsford. He helped me buy the salon.

I'm not sure I'd have done it without him. And I have a sister, Stella — she's in London at the moment, learning the hotel business from the bottom up. She hopes to eventually manage one, maybe even own one of her own. Though I think that might be a bit of wishful thinking.' She smiled fondly. She missed her sister too. Sometimes she thought that the death of her mother had been what had led to the fracturing of the family. Lexie didn't think Stella would have left Adlington if their mother had lived. 'And that's it, really. We're not a large family. Both my parents were only children, and both sets of grandparents died several years ago.'

Bruno's gaze then was a searching one. It was as if he really was trying to see inside her head. Without removing his eyes from her, he asked, 'And your partner — what does he do? When he's around, of course.' The final few words were spoken with more than a trace of irony.

Lexie disregarded that and said, 'Various things. He was in the building trade for a while. Then he worked in a hardware store, and eventually tried his hand at selling insurance. That's what he's doing at the moment. Well, he would be if he was here.'

She'd actually rung his office and asked to speak to him, but the man who'd answered the phone had sounded extremely annoyed. 'He's not here and we haven't seen him for well over a week now.' So she'd ended up no wiser as to where Danny could be. All she did know was that when — if — he decided to return, he'd most likely find himself out of work as well as homeless, because she'd become increasingly angry about his lack of any sort of consideration for her and had more or less decided to end their relationship for good.

To her relief, Ruthie came back into the room, bearing a tray which she set on the huge sideboard next to the table, and putting an end to what was fast turning into an uncomfortable conversation, at least as far as Lexie was concerned. Ruthie then removed their empty plates and replaced them with large oval ones.

A fillet steak in a red wine sauce, with tiny whole shallots and finely sliced red peppers, sat on each. Next she laid out dishes of vegetables for them to help themselves from.

'This looks delicious,' Lexie said.

'It's my own recipe. I call it Steak Adlington.' Ruthie grinned and wished them bon appétit before swiftly leaving the room again.

A dessert of whole pears poached in champagne with thick Cornish cream came next. This was followed by an extensive cheese board, accompanied by purple grapes, beautifully sliced and cored apples, and finely cut sticks of celery, before they finally drank cups of perfectly made cappuccino coffee.

Lexie slumped back in her chair, rubbing her stomach and beaming with pleasure. 'That was the best meal I've ever eaten.'

'Good.' Bruno beamed back. 'Ruthie is a magnificent cook. I tell her she should open her own restaurant — I'd even back her — but she says she's perfectly happy here, and I'm not arguing with that. I'd hate to lose her. She's a godsend when I have to entertain.'

'Do you do that very often?'

'Entertain? Yes, pretty often. I conduct a lot of my business over Ruthie's meals. I tell her it's her cooking that swings it for me.' He laughed. 'Right — shall we return to the snug and have a liqueur? Or a brandy, if you prefer?'

'Oh, no. Any more to drink and I'll be passing out.'

'Really?' He looked intrigued now. 'I can always put you to bed upstairs. We have plenty of room, after all.'

'Oh, I'm not that bad,' she confidently assured him, only to get up from the table and immediately begin to gently sway.

Bruno was at her side instantly. He caught hold of her, sliding his arm about her waist as he did so. 'Come on, I'll help you,' he murmured — seductively, it seemed, to Lexie's sensitive hearing.

As much as she wanted to push his hand away from her waist, she felt too unsteady to risk it. And within seconds, she was being settled onto the settee — where, to her utter dismay, he joined her.

'Some more coffee, I think, don't you?' He lifted up the phone that sat on a small table alongside the settee and said, 'Ruthie, could we have some more coffee? Would you mind?'

Lexie assumed that this particular phone was connected to the kitchen. A useful device, she irritably decided, when he had a woman with him. He didn't have to leave her, not even for a second.

Ruthie appeared almost at once with a pot of coffee, which did seem to confirm Lexie's theory that this was something Bruno made a habit of doing. The house-keeper must keep a pot already prepared. It was pretty well typical, she decided, of a man like him. Who else would entertain a woman by utilising Ruthie's expertise in the kitchen as a form of seduction? She mentally snorted her scorn. No wonder he didn't want to lose her.

Well, if he planned on working his wiles on her, he could think again. No matter how intoxicated she was, she had no intention of becoming yet another of his conquests.

With that in mind, she accepted the coffee that Bruno poured for her and drank it straight down. Almost at once, she felt better — which was just as well, because Bruno was still at her side, his one ankle propped on his other knee, his arm placed along the back of the settee behind her head. He'd only have to move an inch or two to be holding her and kissing her. Shakily, she replaced her cup on its saucer on the low table in front of them.

'Better?' he asked.

'Heaps,' she replied. 'And now, I think I'd better go.'

'Not yet,' he throatily murmured.

She swivelled her head to look at him and found herself staring directly into a pair of smouldering eyes. Without her noticing, he'd managed to inch closer to her. He lifted his hand, and with his index finger beneath her chin, tilted her head backwards.

'I've really enjoyed today, Lexie. I want to see more of you; much, much more.' He spoke softly; huskily.

'Bruno ...' she began to protest, but it was futile. As much as she tried to resist, she found herself yearning for his kiss, every bit as much as he evidently wanted to kiss her. When his head moved the couple of inches necessary, she involuntarily parted her lips in readiness. She heard his low groan, and then he was kissing her passionately, almost savagely, as his arms went round her, pulling her close, pressing her breasts almost painfully against him.

10

In that revealing second, Lexie knew she was perilously close to falling in love with Bruno Cavendish, and there seemed to be nothing she could do to prevent it.

Her breathing quickened as she responded to his kiss. Without removing his mouth from hers, he swivelled her round and then pressed her backwards until she was lying beneath him. He cradled the back of her head in his palm, threading his fingers through her hair as his other hand began to caress her. His fingers gently traced the line of her arched throat before moving slowly onwards to touch her breast, his mouth following the pathway his fingers had taken, down over her still-arched throat, to finally rest on the cleavage nestled in the V of her blouse.

She gave a tiny gasp as she felt him begin to undo the buttons and then slide his hand inside. He slipped the strap of her bra down, revealing her breast to his eyes and his touch. Aching with a deep longing, she arched her back, mutely offering herself up to him and his love-making. His hand at once enclosed the fullness that was bared to him, his finger-tips brushing the sensitised peak.

'Oh God, Lexie,' he groaned. 'I —'

But what he was about to say, she would never know, because there was a soft tap on the door followed by Ruthie asking, 'If there's nothing else I can get you, Bruno, I'll be off to bed.'

They sprang apart, Lexie scrabbling to sit upright, at the same time hurriedly straightening her blouse, refastening the buttons and smoothing her dishevelled hair. Bruno simply watched her, his lips quirking at the corners as he struggled to suppress a grin.

'Relax,' he murmured. 'She won't come in if I don't tell her to.'

Lexie's eyes widened at him. So this was a regular occurrence then — him making love to a woman late at night. And in his snug, of all places. Clearly

Ruthie knew only too well not to enter the room. Lexie stiffened as she stared at him. She should have recognised how skilled he was in the art of seduction by the practised way he'd swivelled her around, then laid her down beneath him. And without as much as a word of protest, she'd allowed him to do it. She'd allowed him to touch her in the most intimate way, thereby making herself appear cheap and easy. But more than that, she felt used; tarnished. And the worst thing of all was that she'd known full well Bruno Cavendish was a womaniser. Jordan had warned her. She'd just chosen not to believe her. Instead, she'd believed Ben, Bruno's accountant, when he'd assured her that a monk probably had more fun than Bruno. Of course a colleague would rush to defend him. How stupid she'd been. How gullible.

She sprang to her feet, pushing away the hands that had snaked back around her, an unmistakable indication that he was fully prepared to carry on right where they'd left off. Well, he could think again.

'I'll go then,' she blurted. 'It's late. Where's my coat?' She grabbed her handbag from the floor at the side of the settee where she'd left it. She then opened it, scrabbling inside for her car keys before she remembered, in sheer horror, that she hadn't come in her own car. Bruno had picked her up.

He too was now on his feet, looking slightly dazed at the speed with which things were moving. 'Lexie, please. There's no need to rush away. I've told you —'

'Yes, I know.' She ground the words out, disgusted at her own eager complicity in their lovemaking. The feeling of having been callously used was still gnawing at her. 'Ruthie won't come in unless you tell her to,' she savagely echoed his words. 'So clearly, this —' She contemptuously indicated the settee and its crumpled cushions. '— is a regular thing for you with any woman who shows willing. I'm surprised you didn't drag me up to your bedroom. That would have been a far more private place. No risk of being interrupted there.'

Bruno didn't speak for a long moment; he didn't need to. His eyes said it all for him. They narrowed, then darkened dangerously, as his mouth tightened. 'I have never dragged any woman up to my bedroom. And this isn't a regular thing. It was a spontaneous thing. Okay, maybe it got a bit out of hand —'

'I'll say,' Lexie muttered. 'Or then again, maybe not. Your hands were pretty active.'

'Ruthie,' he went on, ignoring her remarks, although his voice was harsh with anger, 'was merely being diplomatic, so as not to disturb.'

Lexie didn't let him finish; her anger now matched his and she couldn't contain it. 'So as not to disturb your —?' Her fury robbed her of the final words.

Bruno's look warned her to be very careful. 'My what?' The two words were cold and heavy with scorn, and told her unequivocally that he knew what she had been about to say.

'Y-your sexual exploits. Adventures,' she blurted, 'or-or whatever you choose to call them.'

He snorted then, not bothering to hide his contempt for her statement, and she had to admit she had sounded more than a little foolish.

'My sexual exploits? Is that what you call a kiss? A sexual exploit?' He gave a mirthless smile. 'You must have led a very sheltered life up till now, in that case.'

Stung by his ridicule of her, she snapped, 'But it wasn't just a kiss, was it? It was more. You admitted that.'

He shrugged as if he really couldn't be bothered to argue with her. And really, she admitted, why should he be? He must have women waiting in line for him. He was good-looking and very wealthy, with a truly gorgeous house to boot. What was there to dislike? She couldn't imagine many women turning him down.

'A little more, yes, but . . .'

Her fury exploded again. 'Yes, well, maybe for you it wasn't very much. Me, I'm not into casual lovemaking with just anyone. And certainly not with the practised womaniser you seem to be.'

She saw instantly that she'd overdone things. His eyes turned almost black as his mouth curled with contempt. 'Just to make things clear, I'm not into lovemaking with 'just anyone' either. And there was nothing casual about what we just did.'

Now it was Lexie's turn to snort her disdain. 'Oh, was there not?'

'No. And for your information — and as I recall telling you once before — I'm not a womaniser. And I'm certainly not in the habit of inviting women back here and having sex with them.'

'That's not what local gossip says,' she scoffed.

'Well you've described it pretty accurately — gossip, from a load of empty-headed people who know nothing about me and with little else to do but blacken people's names and reputations.'

'Huh,' she blurted, 'Jordan will be pleased to know you think her empty-headed.'

'That's not what I meant, and you know it,' he growled.

'Well, whatever you meant, I want to go home, and you …' Her words lamely petered out.

'Quite,' he drily retorted. 'I have to take you. Unless, of course, you'd rather walk than share a car with me, a man you clearly regard as a sexual predator.' He cocked his head and regarded her, his expression one that would have put an iceberg to shame.

'I'll call a taxi.' No way did she want to be beholden to him.

'You damn well won't.' He ground the words out. She swallowed nervously, almost frightened of him at this point. He'd reverted to the man she'd believed him to be in the beginning: arrogant, domineering, utterly self-assured, and determined to impose his will on others, whatever they themselves might want. 'I brought you here, and I'll take you home again. And you can take that look off of your face. I won't be trying to lay a finger on you.'

All of a sudden, Lexie felt bad; really, really bad. They'd had a fantastic day and a delicious dinner, and Bruno had been a charming and considerate companion. She said nothing now, however, because she knew her words would only exacerbate an already difficult, if not embarrassing, situation.

'I'll get your coat.' He swung to stride from the room.

Lexie silently followed him into the hallway and snatched the jacket that he stiffly held out to her before slipping it on. He then opened the front door and, without uttering a word, ushered her out. For her part, she meekly and equally silently followed his lead.

They were more than halfway back before she summoned up the courage to say, 'Thank you for a lovely day. I — and Jennifer — really enjoyed it.'

'Until I blotted my copybook and kissed you.' He didn't as much as glance at her as he uttered the words; words that were heavy with scorn.

'I-I'm sorry,' she whispered miserably. Had she overreacted? It had, after all, been little more than a passionate kiss.

Did he now consider her too immature to bother with? Because, let's face it, she'd acted with all the impetuous foolishness of a young, inexperienced girl.

He swivelled his head and regarded her. His look was a piercing one; uncompromising. 'For what? I'd really like to know. For having kissed me? For having allowed me to make certain … overtures? What?'

'For having reacted rather foolishly.'

'Foolishly?' He gave another snort. She wasn't sure whether it signified amusement or scorn. 'Is that how you describe it? Tell me, Lexie, are you always that prickly, that accusing, if a man kisses you? Even when you encouraged him to do so?'

'I didn't encourage.'

His one eyebrow rose. 'Oh? So how would describe your response; the way you practically offered yourself to me? I'm not totally insensitive. It was more than obvious you wanted what was happening every bit as much as I did. If Ruthie hadn't knocked, how would it have ended, do you think? Would you still have halted things? As far as I could tell, you seemed pretty damned willing to let things go a lot further.' He appraised her quizzically. 'Tell me something — is that how you behave with your partner, what's-his-name?'

'Danny,' she softly said.

'Danny. Does he get the ice maiden treatment if he dares to try and make love to you?'

'No, of course not.'

'Are you sure? Maybe that's why he's left you.'

She widened her eyes at him. She hadn't expected such hurtful cruelty from him. But honesty dictated that she ask herself if he actually had a point. She *had* been cool with Danny for a while. Could that really be why he'd left, rather than because he owed money to someone? But wouldn't he have said something? And why would he have left all of his belongings behind? And then there was the man who appeared to be stalking her. If he was searching for Danny, as she suspected he was, then why? No, there was more to it than mere coolness on her part; a lot more. And Danny hadn't been exactly loving to her, hence her suspicion about the possibility of him having an affair.

'I'm sure it's not,' she said.

Bruno slanted a narrowed gaze at her. 'Well, maybe not.' He seemed to soften then as he took in her ashen-faced, distressed state. 'You're probably right, because until we were abruptly interrupted, you were clearly as engaged as I was, and every bit as passionate.'

Lexie felt the familiar blush staining her face.

'I just want you to know, I'm not in the habit of bringing women home. Maybe at one time, before I was married, I might have done, but not since I've been divorced and had Serena with me.'

And she believed him. It was glaringly obvious that he deeply loved his daughter; and from what she'd witnessed so far, he was a good father.

'Well, maybe I was a bit unfair to you,' she muttered.

'Just a little,' he smoothly agreed.

'I'm sorry.'

'Look.' He brought the car to a halt in front of her house. 'I'm sorry too. Maybe I also overreacted. But the truth is, I'm very attracted to you.' He half turned in his seat so that he could look directly at her and she could also see his face. 'And I genuinely believed that you felt the same way.'

She didn't know what to say at that point, because he was right — she did.

'Lexie?' he murmured. 'Am I right?'

She nodded. 'Yes, but I'm not free.'

'Yes, you are. Danny left you of his own accord, to go walkabout as you phrased it. You're not married; you're not even engaged, are you?'

'No, I'm not, but —'

'Look, let's take it slowly. We've got plenty of time. We're not in our dotages yet.' He smiled gently at her. 'Let's get to know each other properly. But a much more important consideration is that Serena will never forgive me if I let you go.' And with that, he broadly grinned at her.

She couldn't help herself; she smiled back. 'Okay. Slowly does it.'

He tilted his head to one side and asked, 'Is it okay if I kiss you, then? I don't want to be accused of further sexual exploitation.'

'Oh God,' she moaned, 'I'm so sorry.'

His gazed narrowed at her as his eyes took on a provocative gleam. 'So you keep saying. Show me just how sorry you are. Maybe with a kiss? Then I might just about manage to forgive you,' he hoarsely said.

She peered at him from beneath lowered eyelids. It was every bit as provocative a gesture as his gleaming look had been. He laughed triumphantly. 'You little witch. Come here.' He reached out to yank her into his arms. The kiss that followed took their breaths away as it went on and on and on, Lexie's mouth opening willingly beneath the pressure of his lips. His tongue slipped inside, to feast long and slow on the sweetness that he found there.

Eventually, breathing hard, he released

her. 'Wow,' he murmured, 'I'd better go right now, or I won't answer for the consequences.'

Lexie grinned, feeling on top of the world. 'Goodnight then,' she whispered.

Bruno gazed at her for a long, long moment. 'I'll ring you tomorrow.'

She climbed from the car and closed the door quietly behind her.

'I'll wait till you're inside,' he called.

'Okay. Talk to you tomorrow, then.'

So happy was she, she was practically hugging herself as she opened her front door and with a final wave to him went inside.

It was then that she admitted she was in love. Deeply and head over heels. There was no point denying it any longer.

* * *

It was in the early hours of the morning that Lexie was awoken by a noise downstairs. It was only faint, but it had sounded like a drawer closing. The bureau drawer? In the sitting room?

Danny. Was he back?

She used an elbow to prop herself up in bed and listen. But when she heard nothing further, she decided she'd been dreaming and lay back down and closed her eyes. She must have slept again until she was awoken for the second time by the click of the front door closing.

She leaped out of bed calling, 'Danny? Is that you?'

She grabbed her dressing gown from the chair to one side of the bed, slipped her arms into it, and then ran out of the room, still calling, 'Danny —?'

She ran down the stairs and into the sitting room. Then she stopped dead and stared round the room.

It wasn't Danny who'd been here, but someone else. Someone who'd literally trashed the place. Someone who, from the sound of the door closing behind them as they left, must have also gained access that way. There'd been no sound of a break-in; and if the intruder had smashed a window to get in, surely she'd have heard it. But why on earth hadn't she heard them creating this mess? They must have worked quickly and in complete silence, apart from the one small sound that she'd heard, and then the click of the front door as they left.

All Lexie knew was that Danny would never have done this. The entire contents of the bureau were scattered over the floor, as were the contents of the cupboard next to the fireplace, mostly books. Cushions had been stripped from the furniture and thrown onto the carpet, presumably to see what lay beneath. Armchairs were turned upside down. A couple of vases were also upturned on the floor.

She went to the window that looked out onto the street and peered through. Whoever the intruder was, they'd only been gone for a matter of moments, so they couldn't have got far. But no matter how keenly Lexie stared up and down the street, she could see no one.

She went into the hallway. The front door was securely closed, but on the doormat were several clumps of what looked like fresh mud. It proved her theory that the intruder entered and then left this way.

She continued into the kitchen and saw the same scene of devastation in there: cupboard doors open, their contents spread over the floor, drawers all emptied. Even the oven and fridge doors were standing open. It was the same scene when she went upstairs to the guest bedroom: the bed had been stripped, the mattress removed. In fact, the whole house had been thoroughly searched — apart from her bedroom, that was. So the intruder must have known she was in there. Her skin crawled at the notion that they might have come in and dragged her from her bed and hurt her, maybe, to make her tell him what she knew of Danny's whereabouts. All she could think was that, mercifully, common sense must have got the better of them, because there was a vast difference in the eyes of the law between simply breaking and entering and actually physically harming someone.

Lexie stood with her brow wrinkled as

she considered what had happened. The intruder had definitely been looking for something; something that Danny was in possession of. Something that must surely belong to whoever the man was that she'd seen outside. It was unlikely to be money. Danny wouldn't have left sufficient to repay a large debt lying around here; he would have taken it with him. So what was it? For the first time, Lexie found herself wondering whether Danny had got himself involved in some sort of drugs ring.

Knowing it would probably be a waste of time, but determined to do it anyway, she rang the police. They did eventually turn up; but just as she'd anticipated, they had a very quick look round, sympathised with her about the mess, and then when she told them that nothing seemed to be missing, quickly lost interest — just like last time.

She didn't bother returning to bed once they'd left again. She knew she wouldn't be able to sleep; she was far too strung out and tense. Instead she sat in the sitting room, drinking cup after cup of tea until after what felt like an eternity, dawn broke. When eight o'clock finally arrived, she rang Jordan at home and asked her to open the salon. Then she rang a locksmith, asking to have her ordinary Yale lock replaced that morning with something not so easily meddled with; a mortise lock of some sort. She also asked if he would fit bolts on the door, top and bottom. That would stop whoever it was targeting her — at least, she hoped it would. Though as the intruder had already proved extremely adept at opening a door without a key, chances were they'd find another way in. A window wouldn't be any sort of barrier, not to someone like that. So maybe some window locks were in order, too.

The locksmith arrived promptly at nine o'clock. Lexie had just opened the door to him when her phone rang. It was Jordan.

'The salon's been broken into — again!' she wailed. 'The place has been completely turned over. Everything's on the floor; it's a mess. But just like last time, I don't think anything's actually been taken. And what's more, whoever it was didn't have to break the glass. They unlocked the door and simply walked in!'

11

Could things get any worse? Lexie reflected. Logic suggested that the intruder in the salon had to have been the same person who'd broken in here. They'd obviously picked the lock there too. Whoever it was must be truly desperate to find something — but what? Again she wondered if it could be drugs-related. Maybe Danny kept a stash somewhere to sell, and then instead of paying his supplier for it — the man who was stalking her, say — he'd done a runner with the money. If that was true, then it could be a huge amount that he owed. That particular theory seemed horribly plausible all of a sudden. In any case, Lexie was starting to run out of explanations for his disappearance. She was even beginning to wonder if he could be dead. These gang bosses could be extremely dangerous. You heard of drive-by shootings all the time.

She sighed. She was doing it again — dwelling on Danny's whereabouts and possible fate. She had to stop it; it was getting her nowhere. She had a business to run, and there was no legitimate reason to suppose he'd come to harm. Sooner or later he was bound to turn up, to collect his belongings if nothing else. She had to make herself believe that.

Once the locksmith had done his work, and had promised to return the following day to fit locks on the windows, Lexie went to the salon and began to clear up with Jordan. She didn't mention the break-in at home or her growing fears for Danny's well-being, just as she didn't ask Alice to help. She couldn't face all the grumbling that would undoubtedly ensue. And she hadn't bothered to call the police to the salon. What would be the point? With nothing missing yet again, she doubted they'd be interested. They didn't seem very interested in simple burglaries anymore, period. As for Danny's disappearance, they didn't seem interested in that either.

So dispirited was she about it all that she'd left the chaos at home exactly as it was. She'd clear it all up this evening. Lexie sighed. The mere notion of it made her feel worn out, and that was before she'd even begun her day's work.

She was in the process of perming the hair of one of her regular clients when the salon phone rang. She left it to Mel to take the call as she usually did. She heard her asking, 'Good morning. Clever Cuts. How may I help you?' before calling to Lexie, 'It's for you!'

'Would you excuse me for one moment?' Lexie asked her client. She walked over and took the phone from Mel. 'Hello?'

'Lexie, it's me, Bruno. Someone has just mentioned that your salon's been broken into again.'

Good heavens, she mused, *that didn't take long. The town's telegraph system must be in full working mode.* 'Yes. Who told you?'

'I was talking to a business associate and he said his wife mentioned it.

She'd just been in and had her hair done — Sylvia Hudson? And in case you're wondering why he bothered telling me ...'

She had been doing exactly that, wondering if he'd told someone about her and their burgeoning relationship. More proof of his mindreading abilities?

'... he asked if I'd been broken into again as well.'

'I see,' she murmured.

'Did they take anything this time?'

'That's the strange thing — no. They left a terrible mess that Jordan and I are in the process of clearing up.' She paused, undecided whether to say anything about the break-in at home. But then, oh what the hell. She needed to tell someone, and when all was said and done, who better than Bruno? He'd probably take it more calmly than Jordan would, and the last thing she needed was her friend panicking about it. It would simply intensify her own feelings of insecurity.

She spoke quietly, not wanting anyone else to overhear. 'Whoever it was got into my house last night too. They ransacked the place, but again, nothing's missing. It has to be the same person.'

Bruno was silent for a long moment. Then he grimly asked, 'While you were there?'

Oh good Lord, had she done the right thing in telling him? Well, it was too late to retract the words, so she might as well tell him everything. 'Yes. I was asleep. A sound woke me, and by the time I'd got up to investigate, whoever it had been was gone. They could only have got in via the front door, as the windows were all still closed and undamaged. I've had a new lock and top and bottom bolts fitted. It won't be as easy from now on.'

'That sounds as if it's happened before. Has it?' He sounded genuinely appalled.

She hesitated yet again before reluctantly saying, 'Yes, once. And someone has been lurking outside, watching the house presumably.'

'For Christ's sake, Lexie. Have you called the police?'

'Yes, a couple of times, but they don't seem interested. Anyway, I don't think it's me he's after.'

'Oh, well that's a relief.' His tone was heavy with irony. 'So, who do you think he's after then?' He was beginning to sound angry now. With her? Or with whoever had been watching her?

'We-ell, it has to be something to do with Danny. That's who he asks for when he phones.'

'When he phones?' He was practically shouting now. 'How many times has this happened?'

'Two, three.'

'And the police haven't done anything?'

'They simply say there's no evidence. He never steals anything, so I think they believe I'm imagining it all. That, or making it up.'

'Oh, do they? And whether they steal anything or not is beside the bloody point. Have they threatened you?'

'No, not really.'

'Not *really*?' He was beginning to sound more than angry; he was sounding absolutely furious. She didn't respond. 'There's something very odd about all of this.' He fell silent, as if he were turning things over in his mind. 'I'm wondering if it's all connected to — when did Danny disappear?'

'The day before the robbery.'

'Right. And the jewels that were taken have never been recovered. It's a bit of a coincidence that the two things happened at the same time. A robbery of extremely valuable jewellery and Danny goes missing. And your salon was the means of entry into my shop. And then you say there's someone watching you. It can't all be coincidence. These things must be connected.'

'What? You can't be suggesting that Danny is a jewel thief. He wouldn't know where to start.'

'No, but a clever accomplice would. Think about it, Lexie, and put two and two together.'

'And make five? No, no. Danny would never . . .' But would he? He'd been behaving very strangely for a couple of months before he disappeared. Supposing he'd become involved with the wrong people; the sort of people who would plan a jewel theft and then carry it out. You heard of gullible individuals being persuaded into acting as a getaway driver in return for a portion of the proceeds of the theft . . .

No, she refused to believe it. Yet she couldn't help but think that it did make some sort of dreadful sense. He'd disappeared at the right time. What if he had taken part and had somehow managed to get away with some, or even all, of the jewels? Her stalker — burglar — could be the accomplice. He was certainly an accomplished thief. He'd had no trouble with her door locks, both at the house and here in the salon.

She frowned. Yet, the first time the glass in the door had been smashed to allow them to get in — which was odd, if he had the skill to pick locks. Could that have been a ruse to distract her from wondering if it could be Danny behind it? Because Danny could easily have got hold of her key. She was pretty sure he hadn't, though, because it was still in her possession. Jordan had a second one. But that would be the first question the police would ask her — who had access to a key? And when she told them Danny did, their suspicions would focus on him. And, truth be told, Lexie supposed he could have had a copy made, although she didn't know when. As far as she could recall, she'd always known where the key was — on her key ring with the house and car key.

But no matter how firmly she told herself Danny couldn't be involved, the things that were now happening to her told her Bruno was most probably right, and Danny was almost certainly involved. Her stalker could have no other reason to watch her, to try and intimidate her, and to break into both her salon and her home. He must be searching for the stolen jewels — that was the only explanation that made any sort of sense.

'Are you okay, Lexie?' Bruno sounded very concerned. 'Do you want me to come to the salon?'

'No, no. I'll be fine.'

'Okay. Well, give me your mobile number and I'll put it into my phone. I don't know why I haven't had it before this.'

She duly recited it for him, as well as her home number. Her thoughts were churning chaotically. She really didn't want to believe Danny was guilty of theft. But there had been a few occasions over the past two years when his behaviour had been decidedly odd. For example, he'd helped himself more than once to a few of the things at the building site he'd worked at to sell on to various mates who were embarking on house renovations. And he'd sounded positively proud when he'd told Lexie about it. She'd naturally remonstrated with him and he'd replied, 'For God's sake, Lexie, everyone does it.' He'd also insisted on being paid part of his wages in cash in order to pay less tax. And he'd quite often bought goods that were obviously stolen. Again, he'd argued, 'Everyone does it.' When she'd replied 'I don't,' he bitten back, 'No, well, you're a proper Miss Goody Two Shoes, aren't you?'

But, even taking all of that into account, Lexie still found it hard to believe he'd actually take part in a real robbery.

Bruno was speaking again, she realised. 'Can we meet this evening?' he said.

'Um — no, I've got a lot of tidying up to do at home, as you can imagine. The place has been more or less trashed.'

'Jeez! Do you want some help?'

'No, I'd rather do it on my own. I'll have a good clear-out while I'm at it.'

'Okay. Well, you have my mobile number, so call me if you change your mind. Promise?'

'I will, yes.'

She returned to Jordan and the tidying up.

'Who was that?' Jordan asked.

'Bruno Cavendish.'

A gleam of speculation appeared in Jordan's eye as she asked, 'What did he want?'

'Someone had told him about the break-in.'

'Oh yeah. Worried about you, was he?'

'A little.'

'So how was yesterday — you know, at the zoo? You haven't mentioned it.'

'Well, we have been a bit busy.' She knew full she hadn't mentioned it. But she didn't want to tell anyone what had happened between her and Bruno, not even her best friend.

'How did it go?'

'It was fine. It's a good zoo; the animals are kept in massive enclosures.'

'I wasn't asking about the animals. How did you get on with Bruno? That's what I really want to know.'

'Oh. Well, I had dinner with him at his place.'

'You did?' Jordan sounded surprised. 'And?'

'That's it. We had dinner.'

'God, you are so annoying, I could shake you. Did he — you know, make a move on you?'

'He kissed me, if that's what you mean.'

'Come on, Lexie,' she grumbled. 'Is he a good kisser? Did it go any further?'

'Not really.' Lexie shrugged.

'I give up.'

Hallelujah, Lexie mused.

'Ben rang me,' Jordan went on.

'Did he? To ask you out?'

'Yeah.' Jordan danced quickly around the broom she was wielding. 'He's taking me for a meal. He wants to get to know me a bit better.' She smiled with extremely irritating smugness.

'Good. I'm pleased. It's about time you had a man in your life.'

'Yeah, well, it hasn't been for want of trying, I can tell you.' And they both laughed.

Lexie belatedly felt Alice's gaze upon her then. She glanced sideways at her. The younger woman looked thoroughly miserable. She too must be wondering where Danny was, if they had been having an affair. Lexie almost felt sorry for her. So much so, that if she had any inkling at all about where he was, she'd be inclined to tell her.

* * *

By the time Lexie returned home that evening, she was totally exhausted after the day she'd had. Nevertheless, once she'd had something to eat she set about clearing up, determined to restore order to the chaos.

She wasn't even half done when her mobile phone rang. Her heart lurched. Could it be Bruno, to ask how she was coping? She looked at the screen and saw a number she didn't recognise. It wasn't Bruno, then. 'Hello? Lexie Brookes speaking.'

Silence was her only answer. She was on the verge of ending the call when Danny's voice said, 'Lex, it's me.'

Shock silenced her at first, but then she cried, 'Danny, where the hell are you?'

'I can't tell you. Are you okay? I would guess Rocky's been pestering you, trying to find me.'

'Rocky? Is that his name? Yes, you could say he's been pestering me.'

'I'm sorry. He's someone I foolishly got myself involved with. Anyway, I'm ringing to warn you to be very, very careful of him. He's dangerous — a nutcase; totally crazy. If he gets too close, call the police.'

'If he gets too close? He's already too close. What have you done, Danny?'

But silence was once again the only response she got. Danny had gone. She instantly called him back, but as had happened before, she only got through to an answering service. He hadn't even had the sense to block his number. Furious with him, she cut the call.

And with that, any remaining doubts she still had about Danny's involvement in the jewel theft vanished. Bruno was right. And now Danny clearly believed she was in danger, to the extent that he'd rung her to warn her about this Rocky. And that really set alarm bells ringing.

What should she do? Call the police? Tell them about his warning? Tell them of her and Bruno's belief about his part in the robbery? But then they'd start a manhunt for Danny. Oh God. What should she do? She covered her face with both hands.

Could she really be in danger? Surely Rocky would have realised by this time that she didn't have the jewels, and that she didn't know where Danny was. But supposing he didn't? Danny wouldn't have bothered to ring and warn her if he didn't think she might be at risk. Her heart lurched with terror.

Get on with the tidying up, she told herself. He hadn't tried to hurt her so far, not even when he'd ransacked the place the night before. He'd left her alone, so why would he do anything to her now?

She began putting things back into the bureau, methodically separating the unwanted items as she did so and placing them in a black bin bag. She was fastening it with a plastic tie when her doorbell rang. She stopped what she was doing and listened. It rang for a second time. She went to the window and peered out, hoping it was Bruno and that he'd ignored her refusal of his assistance. She desperately needed company, someone to distract her from all that was happening. Someone to protect her. But she couldn't see anyone.

Agonisingly nervous now, and with a heart that was pounding, she went to the front door. She opened it just a crack — to no avail. It was immediately slammed back at her, knocking her across the hallway and into the opposite wall.

'Right, you bitch,' the man standing there said. 'It's time you and I had a real talk.'

12

Lexie stared at the man standing in front of her, feeling the blood drain from her face as she succumbed to sheer terror. This had to be Rocky, and she'd been stupid enough to open the door and let him in.

Using one foot, he slammed the door shut behind him; and before she had time to even try to compose herself, let alone ring the police, he'd grabbed her by the arm to push her in front of him into the sitting room. He then dragged her to the settee and shoved her backwards down onto it.

'Right,' he snarled, 'you're going to tell me where Danny is. So, start talking.'

She shrank away from him. 'I-I don't know where he is. I told you — several times.'

Her mind began to work frantically. What the hell was she going to do? How was she going to get out of this? He was dangerous, Danny had said; and judging by the expression on the man's face now, she had no trouble believing that. He could well turn violent if she didn't tell him what he was demanding to know. Oh God. He'd clearly believed she was lying when she'd said she didn't know where Danny was.

Think, she told herself. *Bloody think*.

Her mobile phone. She'd slipped it into her trouser pocket after speaking to Danny. She slid her hand into it now and, trusting that she could do this without being able to see the keypad, pressed one of the keys — number nine, the key that would hopefully speed-dial Bruno's number. She half turned her body into the corner of the settee so that Rocky couldn't see what she was doing, and prayed that Bruno would answer and somehow hear what was going on. If he didn't . . .

But Rocky leant over her, twisting her back to face him, his expression one of menace. 'Don't even think of screaming, or making any noise at all, or else I'll be forced to take certain steps — and believe me, you don't want me to do that. Now, are you going to tell me, or do I have make you?'

She stared up at him as her heart pounded so hard she truly believed it was about to explode from her chest. Her throat was dry; in fact, it hurt as she struggled to speak. 'I-I d-don't know where Danny is!' she loudly cried, praying that Bruno would be listening. She wasn't even sure she'd connected with his number. She hadn't heard any sound of ringing.

'Liar,' Rocky growled. He slapped her across the face; a hard, stinging slap that rocked her head to the side. 'And that's just a taste of what I'll do if you don't talk. You've heard of waterboarding, I'm sure. Don't make me do that to you. I believe it's most unpleasant.'

'Please,' she gasped. 'I can't tell you what I don't know. Danny disappeared right before the jewellery theft in the shop next door to my salon. I haven't seen him since.' She stared at him. *Keep him talking*, she told herself. *Ask questions. Anything to distract him from trying to hurt me. Give Bruno time to get here. Please, please*, she mutely pleaded, *let him be listening*. 'Was that you and Danny?'

'What do you think? The bastard was supposed to take the jewellery to his car and wait for me. I was a bit slow getting through the hole in the wall — and-and he drove away, leaving me high and dry.' He actually looked embarrassed as he said this.

Lexie had already noticed his broad girth, so she had no trouble imagining that in his haste to escape the scene of the crime he might have had a spot of trouble. The hole hadn't been that large.

'And I haven't seen or heard from him since,' he went on. 'I don't believe he hasn't been in touch with you, so you're going to tell me where he is. He must have the stuff with him, because it's certainly not here. Or at your salon.'

Lexie again said, 'I'm telling you the truth — I have no idea where he is. I haven't heard from him. Don't you think I would tell you if I had? Please . . .' Her eyes stung with tears now as sickening dread took hold of her. There was a look of such rage on his face that she wouldn't be surprised if he killed her. In fact she fully expected him to, because she sure as hell couldn't tell him what he wanted to know.

'I don't believe you,' Rocky bit out. His gaze narrowed as he leant nearer. His breath stank of tobacco. He gave Lexie a humourless grin, baring teeth that were stained brown. She shrank back even further into the corner of the settee, trying desperately to get as far away from him as she could.

All of a sudden, his hand shot out and grabbed her around the throat. 'If you don't tell me right now, I'm going to squeeze this pretty little neck of yours until you pass out. Then I'll revive you and do it all over again until you talk. So do yourself a favour.'

'No!' she screamed. 'Please — I can't tell you!'

'Liar,' he said. He put both hands around her throat and started to squeeze. She tore at his fingers, scratching his skin as she frantically fought to free herself. It was useless; he was too strong. His grip on her tightened. She struggled to breathe. Oh God, she couldn't … The room and everything in it started to dim around her. 'Ple-ease …' And then it all went black.

She was brought round again by several stinging slaps on her face, and then Rocky took hold of her shoulders and shook her hard. Her head rocked back and forth this time, making her fear that her neck was about to snap.

'I see you're back with me, then.' His expression was pure evil. 'Now that I've proved I'm a man of my word, start talking.'

'D-don't you th-think I would if-if I could? I-I can't tell you.'

'Fine.' His fingers tightened round her throat again, and again she fought to free herself as she wildly struggled for breath. 'No, no,' she moaned. But he didn't stop.

She felt her consciousness slipping away once more. Her last thought was that he was going to kill her, before darkness descended for the second time.

He slapped her awake again. 'I won't stop until —'

A loud banging sounded on the front door, startling them both. It was enough to make Rocky release her. But before he could make any attempt to escape, several men's voices shouted, 'Police — open up now!'

There came the sound of the door being kicked open, and several policemen leaped into the room. Bruno was right behind them.

'Oh, thank God — you heard me!' Lexie gasped when she saw him. Finally, the tears began to stream uncontrollably. She lifted both hands to her face as sobs shook her.

One of the policemen took hold of Rocky, forcing his hands down behind him, before he swiftly fastened a set of handcuffs onto him, at the same time informing him of his arrest and cautioning him. As for Bruno, he strode straight to Lexie. He pulled her up from the settee, where she was still weeping, and straight into his arms.

'Sweetheart, are you okay? Has he hurt you?'

'Y-you heard me,' she again said.

'I did, thank God. I called the police straight away, and amazingly here we are. I'll never say another word against them. They're marvellous people, all of them. Did he hurt you?' He held her away from him then, his narrowed gaze keenly scrutinising her, looking for any signs of injury.

'Just a bit of a slap, that's all,' she said in a small voice. *Understatement of the year.*

He lifted his hand and tilted her head backwards, and his gaze dropped to her throat. 'My God, he tried to throttle you!'

'Yes,' she confessed, and softly wept. 'I was so scared. I blacked out twice.'

He held her tightly against him. 'You're safe now,' he tenderly murmured. 'I've got you. Sssh. You're okay.'

She lifted her head and stared up at him. 'You were right — it was him and Danny who took your jewels. Danny managed to run off with them, and that's why Rocky's been so keen to find him.'

'Ms Brookes,' one of the policemen said — he'd obviously been listening to her, 'do you have any idea where this Danny is?'

'Danny Blake,' she told him. 'I don't. He rang me a while ago to warn me about Rocky. Him.' She pointed at the snarling man as he was being dragged away. 'But he rang off before he could tell me where he was. Sorry. I do have his mobile number though, if that's any use.'

'It certainly will be. Our experts will track him down, don't you worry. But for now we've got one of them, and that's better than neither. Now, if you feel up to it, we'll need a statement from you.'

* * *

When they were finally alone again, Bruno took Lexie into his arms once more. First he closely examined her face and throat. 'I think we should go to A and E and get you checked over.'

'No, I'm fine. Really. I'm a little sore, but that'll pass.'

'Are you sure?' His face was as pale now as hers as the shock of it all sank in. 'He could have killed you, Lexie. Thank God I heard it all, or most of it. Where was your phone? It was all a bit muffled.'

'In my trouser pocket.' She smiled shakily. 'It was all I could think to do. Anyway, he didn't hurt me — well, at least not much, thanks to you.'

'I very nearly had a heart attack once I realised what was going on. I rang the police and told them it was a matter of life and death — which it clearly was.' His face darkened. 'Tell me exactly what Danny said.'

'He warned me to be careful of Rocky; that he was dangerous and crazy, which I can't argue with now.'

He pulled her even closer to him, so close she could feel the pounding of his heart against her. 'I could have lost you,' he groaned. 'Oh, my love.' And he bent his head to hers, capturing her lips, gently prising them open and then kissing her with heart-aching tenderness.

Lexie slipped her arms up and around his neck, responding with everything that was in her. He moved with her and, still holding her close, sank down onto the settee, where he began to make love to her, his mouth gently moving all over her face and her throat, his hands caressing tenderly, until all of a sudden he abruptly stopped.

She gazed up at him, her expression one of vulnerability and uncertainty. 'What's wrong?'

'If I carry on with this, I won't be able to stop, and now's not the right time.'

'Why not?'

'You're hurt; bruised. I don't want to make that worse.'

'You won't,' she murmured. 'Please — don't stop.'

He stared at her, his concern for her only too evident. 'Are you sure?'

She nodded. 'I-I want — need — you

to make love to me.'

'Oh Christ, Lexie,' he groaned.

'Please.'

But he needed no further bidding. He began to kiss her again, this time with passion. Lexie responded with equal ardour, as their lovemaking transported her into a rapture she'd never experienced before.

It was some time later when they lay in each other's arms, still exchanging butterfly-light kisses, that Bruno said, 'I love you so much.'

'I love you too.'

He covered her in kisses again before he said in a low voice, 'You can't stay here, not on your own.'

'It's okay. Rocky's been arrested.'

'But what if Danny decides to come back?'

'That's highly unlikely. He's got what he wants — your jewels. He won't show his face here again. He'll know the police will be waiting to arrest him if he does. I'll be perfectly safe.'

'Maybe.' He gazed at her for a long moment. 'But Lexie, I need to say something.'

She widened her eyes at him.

'Jeez! Don't look at me like that. I turn to mush every time you do it.'

'Really? You look pretty solid to me.' She grinned at him.

'Be serious, woman, and listen to me. You know that Serena adores you. I adore you. I have from the first second I saw you poking your head out of a doorway to look at me. I fell in that instant — hook, line and sinker. So I want us to get married. We can get a special licence. But until then, I want you to move in with us now, tonight.'

'Bruno, hang on.' Lexie pulled slightly away from him, the better to see his face, and the expression in his eyes. 'You barely know me. It's only been — what? Not even a couple of weeks. We can't.'

Anguish filled his eyes at that. 'You said you love me. Or did I mishear?'

'No, you didn't. I do love you. But we mustn't rush into this. You said so yourself. Take it slowly, you said. Get to know each other.'

'Okay. Okay. Well, at least move into the manor. We'll really be able to get to know each other then, though I already feel I know almost everything about you. But most of all, I'll know you're safe. Of course ...' He gave her a shaky smile. 'The real truth is, I can't live without you. I don't *want* to live without you. I've never been more sure of anything.'

'Oh, Bruno.' Lexie gazed into his eyes. They were blazing with love and passion. 'Okay, I'll move in — but separate bedrooms.' She ignored his look of startled dismay. 'At least to start with. And let's make it tomorrow evening. There's a few things I need to do here first.' Not least, she mused, to pack her belongings. 'And I have to go to the salon tomorrow.'

'Okay. I'll agree to anything just to have you with me. But ... oh God.' A look of anguish crossed his face. 'I'm sorry, but I'll have to leave you now and go home. Ruthie's supposed to be meeting someone; a friend. She said she was happy to stay with Serena when she knew what was happening here; but if I go now, she can still retrieve something of the evening. I'm not leaving you alone, though; so if you won't come with me, I'm getting one of my security men to park outside. He'll keep an eye on things.'

* * *

The next morning, Lexie went to the salon. Jordan was already there; she'd unlocked again as Lexie was late arriving. She regarded her friend with concern. 'You look strange, Lex. Is everything okay?'

'It is now.' She proceeded to tell Jordan all that had happened the previous evening. That Danny had been one of the thieves who'd broken into Cavendish Gems and had then absconded with the stolen jewels. That his accomplice had been stalking her and had finally burst into the house and threatened to kill her. How Bruno and the police had rescued her. She concluded by telling her she was moving into the manor with Bruno that evening; that they loved each other and planned to marry eventually. And throughout it all Jordan stood, mouth open; and for the first time since Lexie had known her, she was totally speechless.

Finally she managed in shock, 'Bloody hell, Lex. You don't believe in doing things by halves, do you?'

'You can say that again.'

'Bloody.'

'Yeah, yeah, okay. Look, I must have a word with Alice. There's something I think she should know.'

Alice had been watching Lexie and Jordan intently. It was obvious she'd guessed by their demeanour that something was up.

'Alice,' Lexie said, 'can we have a word in the staffroom?'

Alice, looking decidedly nervous at that, mutely did as Lexie asked. Once Lexie had closed the door behind them, she turned to her and said, 'There's something I think you'd want to know.' She quickly told her about the call from Danny. 'I don't think he'll be back, Alice.'

Alice looked stricken, her face pale, and tears sprang into her eyes.

'You love him, don't you?'

Alice nodded. 'Yes,' she whispered. 'And he said he loved me, though we'd only been out three or four times.' She gave Lexie a sheepish look. 'Sorry.'

'Don't be. I'd guessed as much; and to be truthful, Danny and I haven't been close lately.'

'I know; he said. Look, I think it's best if I find a job somewhere else.'

'It might be, yes. You can work out your month's notice while you look around for something.'

'Thank you. I'll be as quick as I can.'

* * *

That evening after Lexie returned home, a feverish excitement assailed her as she piled what belongings she could into her car and made the short journey to the manor house. She'd sort out her house and the rest of her things, as well as the termination of her rental agreement, and all of Danny's belongings, at some later date. For now, she needed to be with Bruno.

Serena was waiting in the doorway for her. Ruthie was standing with her. 'She wanted to be out here at seven o'clock this morning, but I told her you'd probably have to go to work first. So we managed to wait until —' The housekeeper checked her wristwatch. '— oh, half an hour ago.' She smiled indulgently down at the little girl before looking back at Lexie and saying, with a frown of anxiety, 'Are you okay? Bruno told me what happened.'

Lexie nodded. 'Yes, I'm fine.'

'Oh, that is good news. But if there's anything at all I can get you, please just ask. Now, I've prepared the pink room for you, so — ah, here's Bruno. I'm sure he'll want to show you where everything is.'

'Lexie,' he murmured, pressing his lips to hers as he enfolded her in his arms. 'Darling, it's so good to see you again. I've missed you.'

She grinned. 'Yes — after all, it's been so long since last night.'

'To me it's felt like an eternity,' he whispered. 'So, come on; let's fetch your things from the car and get you settled.'

'Can I come too, Daddy?' Serena pleaded.

'Okay, but it's nearly bedtime. We'll have to be quick.'

Bruno lifted Lexie's luggage from the boot of her car, leaving the various boxes she'd placed in the rear seat until later. He then led the way up the stairs, Serena following with the small box she'd insisted on bringing, and chattering excitedly at Lexie's side.

The room he showed her into was the most luxurious Lexie had ever been in, with its four-poster bed, a complete wall of wardrobes, and a large vanity unit. There was a flat-screen television, two armchairs, and even a bookcase. There was also a small fireplace.

'Is this okay?' he anxiously asked as he set the cases down on the floor. 'There's an en-suite through there.' He pointed to a door that Lexie hadn't noticed till then.

'Is it *okay* —?' she breathed. 'It's

wonderful. I could fit my entire house into it. In fact, I could live in it."

'Could you, now?' He slanted a glance at her. 'Well, I have to tell you, I have other plans for you. Anyway, it's yours — although,' he murmured into her ear, 'not for long, I hope. I've felt for a while now — well, for the past couple of weeks or so — that the master suite is too big for one person. It definitely needs two. And I can't wait too long to have you in my bed, so I'm warning you — I'm not a patient man.'

Desire, hot and urgent, gleamed from him at Lexie, thrilling her so much that her whole body flamed. For the truth was, she also couldn't wait. She didn't say anything, though. Serena was with them, after all. And it hardly seemed decent to move straight into the master bedroom. But if the way she was feeling at the moment was any sort of guide, then the master bedroom most certainly wouldn't be his alone for long.

The three of them then had an early supper, and then Bruno and Lexie together put Serena to bed. Once she was tucked under the duvet, the little girl held her arms out to Lexie, who bent down and lavished kisses upon her satin-smooth cheeks. 'I'm so glad you're going to live with us, Lexie,' she whispered. 'We can be a proper family now. But Daddy ...' She frowned at her father. '... why is Lexie in a different bedroom to you?'

Lexie swallowed a laugh as she decided to leave it to Bruno to answer that one.

He had no problem, as it turned out. 'Well, I hope she won't be for long, but it's up to Lexie.'

As Lexie met his pleading glance, she silently conceded that it probably wouldn't be long at all.

In fact, the separate rooms didn't even last for that night. She desperately wanted to be with Bruno; longed to have him make love to her again, just as he had last evening.

Deciding to surprise him, she got ready in her own room. But then, with a heart that was belatedly pounding with a mixture of nervousness and churning desire, she walked along the landing to Bruno's bedroom.

He looked up, startled, as she opened the door and walked in. His eyes widened even further as he took in the diaphanous mid-thigh-length nightdress that she'd dashed out and bought that morning. And then he simply held his arms out to her. She moved quickly to the bed and sank into them.

'Lexie, my love,' he breathed. 'You've come.'

And as his mouth covered hers, and his arms enfolded her, Lexie knew that finally she'd found her true love. Everything, and everyone else, was forgotten.

Other titles in the
Linford Romance Library:

LOVE IN A MIST

Margaret Mounsdon

Minnie Hyde — flame-haired beauty and acclaimed actress of her day — leaves a legacy of confusion when she dies without a will. Penny Graham, a single parent running a pet-grooming parlour in a disused theatre on the land, is soon threatened with eviction by Minnie's grandson, Roger Oakes. That is, until long-lost Australian granddaughter Sarah Deeds also lays claim to the estate. Amidst the confusion, Penny must deal with her growing feelings for a man who would make her homeless . . .

THE DANCE OF LOVE

Jean Robinson

Starting a new phase in her life after the death of her chronically ill mother, Carrie decides to go on a cruise to Alaska. All the other passengers seem to be in couples, though, and she immediately feels left out. Then she meets fellow lone passenger Tom, who becomes a firm friend — until the handsome and elusive Greg steals her heart. Should Carrie take a chance on him, or accept the security offered by Tom? And what will happen when the cruise comes to an end?

SHEARWATER COVE

Sheila Spencer-Smith

When her cousin asks for help with running his holiday business in the Isles of Scilly, Lucy Cameron is happy to oblige. On the ferry there, she meets Matt Henderson, an attractive local marine biologist — but is appalled by his work. Soon the sea air, soft sands, and friendly locals make Lucy feel welcome; and as she gets to know Matt, she's tempted to see him in a better light. Lucy's stay at Polwhenna is temporary, though — and as the time to go home creeps closer, she is increasingly torn . . .

ROSES FOR ROBINA

Eileen Knowles

Brett had been the love of Robna's life — until he disappeared without a word. But now he's back in Little Prestbury, to attend his brother's funeral and take on the running of the family estate. And Robbie has to work with him . . . How will her boyfriend Richard react — and how will she cope? Despite telling anyone who'll listen — herself included — that she's over Brett, Robina just can't seem to stop thinking about him . . .

A LOVE DENIED

Louise Armstrong

1815: Felix, Earl of Chando, sets out to engage a suitable companion for his much-loved mother. He finds her in Miss Phoebe Allen, whose charm and good nature win him over. Once at Elwood, Phoebe also takes on the muddled household accounts, and advises Felix on how he can save the ailing estate. Felix finds himself falling in love with her — but he is determined never to marry, as he fears there is bad blood in his family. Will Phoebe change his mind?